WHERE THE HELL
IS TESLA?

WHERE THE HELL IS TESLA?

A NOVEL

BY ROB DIRCKS

GOLDFINCH PUBLISHING

Published by Goldfinch Publishing
An Imprint of SARK Industries, Inc.
www.goldfinchpublishing.com

Publisher's Note:
This is a work of fiction. Names, characters, places, and incidents either are the product of the author's imagination or are used fictitiously. Any resemblance to actual persons, living or dead, events, or locales is entirely coincidental. Use of Nikola Tesla as historical figure and character have been approved by William Terbo, grand nephew and last living relative of Tesla.

Library of Congress Cataloging-in-Publication Data
Rob Dircks, 1967-
Where the Hell is Tesla? / by Rob Dircks
p. cm.
ISBN 978-0-692-60809-8

Print editions manufactured in the USA

Praise for *Where the Hell is Tesla?*

"If Bill and Ted were approaching middle age (and gotten just *this much* more world weary along the way), then went on an Even More Excellent Science Fact Adventure, you might get something like Rob Dircks' debut novel, *Where the Hell is Telsa?* Smart, funny, and just like its titular scientist, impressively inventive, this is a must-read for anyone who aced science and, even more so, for those of us who didn't. Which means, quite simply, it's a book for everyone."

– Michael Zam, Screenwriting Professor, NYU

"Reminds me of Vonnegut. Yeah, I said that."
– Ruth Sinanian, connoisseur of fine literature

Amazon Reviews:

"An extraordinarily unexpected delight… will appeal to fans of Pratchett and Adams."

"A wild, witty wonderful ride through a historically accurate backdrop. You will laugh, it's not dumb humor but very smart."

"Very entertaining and a great homage to a great scientist. If you're looking to laugh out loud while reading, then this is the book for you."

"I was laughing at times and on the edge of my seat other times. The character of Chip is wonderful."

"I advise all readers to not attempt to read this before bed or a nap thinking you will read just one chapter. You won't and you can't!"

Part One
The Journal

CHIP'S OFFICIAL DISCLAIMER:

The events depicted in the following emails did not happen.
I have never been in contact with a covert government
group attempting to suppress knowledge of the lost journal
of Nikola Tesla. I have not been threatened with death if
I divulge the secrets contained inside. They did not buy
me this handsome jacket (oh shit, you're reading this –
trust me, it looks great). They did not come to my place,
and liquor me up, and offer to publish this book as a sci-fi
comedy novel to throw the public off the trail of the real
truth.

Or did they?

I'm kidding. Of course they didn't.

Or did they?

God, I can't keep my big mouth shut.

1
Today at "Work"

From: Chip Collins
To: Pete Turner
Date: May 27, 2015 9:02pm
Subject: today at "work"

Yo dude,

Something weird/cool happened today at work. I found this crazy book.

Wait, let me back up. After all the drug tests, physicals, psych evaluation, blah, blah, blah, I couldn't wait to sit on my ass and do nothing. It's a security guard job, right? I'm not even working for the FBI – just a contractor, watching this old research building until it gets demoed for new condos or some shit.

But they don't even give me a desk. An office, sure, but literally nothing in it. Not a single tack in the wall. Nothing. So I'm guessing I'm supposed to stand there all day. STAND. Dude, there is NOBODY around, and I'm going to stand at attention? Screw that. So I ask Ted (he's the FBI guy who comes by in the mornings) if I can have a desk and a chair. "Sure, slacker." I mean, he didn't say it, but he might as well have. Dick.

So he takes me into the bowels of this place – it's HUGE, dude – and I'm thinking "I'm supposed to walk this whole thing every day? Right." I'm looking around, I can't believe how long this hallway is we're walking down, and

Ted stops all of a sudden. So I bump into him, totally by accident, and he glares at me like he's going to pull some FBI karate shit on me or something. I'm all apologies, though, so he relaxes his Bruce Lee stance a little and points at the door in front of us.

"In here."

I know, I know, get to the book. But dude, you had to see what was in this room. I'm talking THOUSANDS of desks, piled up to the ceiling. And this isn't a small room. It's like an airplane hangar. Bigger. A zeppelin hangar. So you've got thousands of desks – the old government issue *survive-a-nuclear-explosion* ones from the fifties – about a million chairs, and I couldn't even guess on the boxes. A jillion, I don't know. Is a jillion a real number? If it is, there were a jillion boxes. So Ted's all smart and he smiles and says "take your pick." So I point to the one on the bottom of a pile of about a hundred just to be a pain in the ass. And he's like "I don't care. It's your back."

Then he leaves, because you know he's got better stuff to do than babysit the security guard at the mothballed research building (I'm getting to the book, trust me), and I pick myself a beauty of a desk. No dents. Minimal scratches. I hump it back to my office (on a dolly – the thing weighs more than a refrigerator full of lead weights) with a chair that still had the leather on it and didn't look like it had been pissed on, or had a hidden spring that could leap out and claw my balls.

Okay, the book. So I'm sitting at my new (ha!) desk, you know, playing around with the drawers, admiring that this thing will clearly still be around in the year three thousand, and I get to the bottom right drawer. It's stuck.

FUCK!

I am NOT going all the way back to get another one. No way. This one is it. But it's bugging the shit out of me that the drawer is stuck. I know security guards don't need even one drawer, but I don't care. I'm pissed. I look around for a tool or something (I don't know why, because there really is NOTHING in the room except this giant desk), and then storm out to my fucking car, angry that it's raining, and that the goddam drawer is stuck, and my car is a piece of shit, and I don't even know if my tools are in the trunk. But they are, so I hustle back in and shake off like a wet dog.

Okay, now we actually get to the book. I take my flathead screwdriver to the drawer (being pretty careful, because this thing really is an object d'art), and eventually wiggle the locking bar or whatever it is enough to pop the drawer open. Pop.

Initially, I'm like "No wonder this thing weighs a million pounds - the entire FBI Old Useless Paperwork Library is in here." But then, since I have nothing to do (except walk the insanely-long halls, which I've already decided I'm never doing), I start looking through the old files and I find the book:

The Journal of Nikola Tesla, 1941-

Dude - there is some WILD shit in there. I can't even tell if it's true or not. You want to hear some of it?

From: Pete Turner
To: Chip Collins
Date: May 27, 2015 11:31pm
Re: today at "work"

Who's Nikola Tesla?

From: Chip Collins
To: Pete Turner
Date: May 29, 2015 9:47pm
Re: today at "work"

Wait - seriously? I mean, I don't know a lot, but you've really never even *heard* of him? TESLA, dude – the electricity guy. Invented alternating current. Invented the radio. Invented radar. Crazy smart geek scientist type.

Well according to Wikipedia (how do you think I knew all this stuff?), he got old and weird, talking about communicating with extraterrestrials and shit. End of story, right?

WRONG.

What they don't say on Wikipedia is what I found in the book. Dude – this badass invented an "INTERDIMENSIONAL TRANSFER APPARATUS." (I know, I know, what the hell is that.) Apparently Tesla was big into waves, waves of all kinds – radio, energy, whatever. And somehow he figured out that you could jump onto a different set of waves – and into a totally different dimension.

So I'm reading this, and I'm like "huh?" I mean, the guy's not exactly explaining down to my reading level in this journal. But this is what I piece together from the book using my caveman brain, Red Bull, and three full days of research while I'm at work (a.k.a. sitting on my ass):

- At any particular moment, an event has infinite possibilities (not "event" like a wedding, "event" like anything, like you going to the fridge for a sandwich)

- Each possibility actually happens, on its own wavelength (I know, you've never heard me use the word "wavelength" before)

- These infinite combinations of event waves create an infinite set of separate, distinct dimensions. (Okay, I copied that one right from the journal.)

WTF, right? Okay, so if you're even more caveman than me (which I think you are), here's an example: let's say you're hungry. You decide to go to the fridge and grab the leftover half a sandwich from Subway. Nom-nom. Done. That's dimension number one.

OR...

you decide that leftover half sandwiches from Subway are for losers, and you deserve a fresh one, so you get in your car and drive to Subway, but on the way, BAM! you get hit by a truck and die. That's dimension number two. Now the poor world of dimension number two is without Pete Turner, who could've been president or invented a cure for cancer (not likely for either of these, but I'm making a point). So you can see (hopefully, because I'm not going into this any more) how screwed up and different things get pretty damn quick – and that was ONE decision by ONE guy about ONE sandwich.

You still with me?

From: Pete Turner
To: Chip Collins
Date: June 2, 2015 10:03pm
Re: today at "work"

Maybe. What kind of sandwich was it?

From: Chip Collins
To: Pete Turner
Date: June 3, 2015 6:22pm
Re: today at "work"

Really? That's your question? Chicken Ranch Melt. I don't know. It doesn't matter.

Listen, dude, get over here NOW. I found something at the end of the journal. I'll call you, too. Get over here.

2
If You Get This,
Call the FBI

From: Chip Collins
To: Julie Taylor
Date: June 4, 2015 5:43am
If you get this, call the FBI

Hi Julie,

Listen, I know I'm a douche. I had no excuse to say what I said, and now I've left you hanging for a couple of months. I'm totally sorry.

But now I really need you.

I don't know if email even works where I am, but you're always my go-to for help, so I figured you're my best shot. It's life or death. (I know how many times have I said that before, but this time I'm serious.) Here's the nutshell:

Me and Pete are trapped in between dimensions and we can't get out.

(Wow, actually typing that makes me realize how stupid it is to think an email from my phone might somehow make it to you. But right now you're the only thing that's standing between barely-holding-it-together Chip and totally-shitting-his-pants Chip, so that's the plan.)

I'll explain, and maybe while you're reading this you can get in touch with the FBI and get us the hell out of here.

You're the best. I love you. (I know, NOW I say I love you, now that I'm desperate and stuck between dimensions. But I was going to say it anyway, I'm just – like I said – a douche.)

Okay, so I've attached my emails to Pete as backstory for you and the feds. (BTW, you may want to remind them that they lost the journal in the first place, so I didn't really steal anything. In fact, a little bonus might be in order once we get out, seeing as we found their book and discovered some pretty earth-shattering shit here. But we can talk about that when we're all safe and sound and at home.)

Caught up? Good.

So Pete comes over to my place, and I show him the last entry in the journal. Well, not right away. First we have a couple of PBRs and play Madden until I kick his ass. He hates that. You know, because he's all great at sports and I can't even throw a football like a third-grade girl, but I can still take him down on the Xbox. Remember that time we were at your place and he got so pissed he tipped over the coffee table? You were laughing so hard you started to choke, and I thought you were dying so I did the heimlich (or my version of it), and you were like "Get the fuck off me, I'm fine!" Then we both cracked up and Pete stormed out.

Okay, now I'm an idiot. I'm sitting here crying into my stupid phone, only now realizing – obviously too late – how much I miss you. If you were here you'd say "awww" (after you slapped me in the face for being a douche).

Sorry. Back to the part where we desperately need your help. So I read Pete the last entry in the journal (using my Serbian accent you love so much):

"7 January, 1943: I, Nikola Tesla, will now enter the INTERDIMENSIONAL TRANSFER APPARATUS, a portal of my invention *(he always puts the name in all caps - it's annoying.)*, located in the back of the closet in the north guest room. I have activated the latch, and have peered inside. Exciting! I will leave this journal for future generations to follow in my footsteps. But first, please tell Mr. Charles on the seventh floor that I will enjoy no longer having to smell his disgusting food aromas. And inform Mrs. Burdge that I will no longer be able to look after Fluffy when she is away on holiday. Goodbye."

You know what I'm thinking, right? It seems stupid now, of course, but I'm thinking we HAVE to check out this INTERDIMENSIONAL TRANSFER APPARATUS (now he's got me doing the all caps). See if it exists, and see if it works. (Spoiler alert: it definitely works! Help!)

Okay, I know I'm getting off track, but you'll love the conversation me and Pete have after reading this:

"So, you want to check this thing out, right?"
"Fuck no. What are you, an idiot?"
"Dude. What could possibly go wrong?"

"Classic. Cut to scene of us in jail. Or scene of us dead. Or scene of us God-knows-where in space-time."

"Well it would be space, not time. It would be the same time no matter where we went. It's a dimension machine, not a time machine. "

"Oh, gee, now I totally want to go."

"Yeah. No time issues. No meeting your older-slash-younger self shit. I don't think."

"Good for you, dude. Have a blast. I'm going home."

So Pete starts heading for the door, and I know I have to pull out the big guns.

"So what, are you a pussy?"

He stops dead, and I know he's considering punching me right in the face. But he never has in fifteen years, and I know he never will, so I go for the jugular.

"You gonna live your life looking good on your surfboard and your old-guy soccer team, pretending to know shit about financial markets or whatever your job is, and never actually DO anything? Huh?"

I got him. I can tell even before he can. He's in. He smiles and walks toward me, with his arms open.

And then he punches me in the face.

Now it's not what you think (or maybe what you would hope under the circumstances) – no knockout, no broken nose with the bloody tissues hanging out of my nostrils, no "fuck-you-our-friendship-is-over" shit. He grazes me – yes, with that perfect football-throwing hand-eye coordination

– just to scare me. But I do fall on my ass, my favorite body part, and it stings (mostly my pride - my ass is cushy enough to survive a fall perfectly fine).

"Whatever. I'm in. But this is the last time I'm letting you talk me into something stupid. Wait. It's always something stupid with you, so forget I just said that. Just don't be a dick."
"Okay, sorry. Promise."

God, I write too much. This email is like twenty pages long already. I'll try to get to the point.

So me and Pete head over to the New Yorker Hotel to check it out. (Tesla lived there in Room 3327. How cool is that? Living in a hotel. Like "Room Service? Send up another Lobster Thermador, my good man!" But he was broke, so maybe it was more like "Room Service? Send up some crackers, my good man!") Of course, we haven't planned this out at all, other than getting there, so the conversation with the girl at the check-in desk goes something like this:

"May I help you?"
"Yes. Ah, we'd like a room. Just for a couple of hours."
She raises her eyebrows, and I immediately know what she's thinking: which one's the prostitute?
"Uh, what I meant to say is, we'd like to visit Room 3327. We're researchers – fans, in fact – of Nikola Tesla. We'd consider it an honor to repose in the room he stayed in."

She eyes me suspiciously, but my knowledge and use of the word "repose" has disarmed her. Apparently prostitutes don't know about Tesla or words like "repose." I'm off the hook.

"Yes, the Tesla Room. I'm sorry, however, rooms are only available for full night stays."

"Uh, sure. We'll take it for one night."

"All right. It is available. The rate is $725."

"We just need one night."

"Yes."

"Fuck. Ah, I mean, Yes. That's fine."

I look at Pete. He's glaring at me. Glaring like he wished he had punched me in the face harder – bloody-tissues-hanging-out-of-my-nostrils harder. He's grinding his teeth, too. But he knows he's the one with the actual job, so he ponies up. (By the way, I have a job now you'd be happy to know. I'm a security guard. Or I was. But in any case it's not really an actual job. But I'm trying.)

Eventually, Pete gets over the money thing, and realizes we're at the door of Room 3327.

"Dude. Do you really think they never found this? That the FBI is a bunch of morons?"

"Uh. Yes. Total morons. Dude, first: they lost this journal, right? So it probably never even got read. Second: they thought he was demented anyway, right? I bet they put first-year Special Agent Lefty Shitforbrains on his case. And third: you think the New Yorker Hotel wanted the FBI in Room 3327 for the infinite future, investigating some INTERDIMENSIONAL TRANSFER APPARATUS? They probably re-did the whole suite the minute the feds left. Coverup."

"The hotel is covering up a portal to other dimensions, so they can rent this room."

"Yup."

"Just yup."

"Yup. It's obvious."

I think this made some perverted kind of sense to Pete, because he willingly follows me into the suite and we head right for the north guest room. (After we figure out which way is north.) I don't know why, but I expected floor-to-ceiling research papers, maybe a big wooden globe, beakers and shit, like Dumbledore's office or something. But no. Typical hotel room. Ugly drapes. Whiny air conditioner. Beige everything. BOOORING.

But we're here for work. We go right to the back of the closet and...

Nothing.

I mean, of course. What did I expect – a big neon sign that said "Interdimensional Transfer Apparatus?" (Except that it would be in all caps.) So me an Pete get into a little married-couple fight. I know you love when Pete gets mad, so here's the transcript:

"I told you this was stupid. The FBI took it."
"You can't TAKE it. It's a passageway. A portal. It's here. But no. You never believe in me."
"What are you, my wife?"
"Fuck that."
"Good. Now we can leave."
"Dude. You just made a mortgage payment to be here. We're not leaving."
"Okay. What do you want to do instead, 'Repose'?"
"That hurt."
"Poor Chip. Who's the pussy now?"

I take a feeble swing at Pete, which of course he easily avoids. So my fist hits the back of the closet wall, and there's this weird metallic sound.

"Dude. Was that a weird metallic sound? Or is sheetrock supposed to sound like that?"

Pete shakes his head, and we stare at the closet wall like a couple of cavemen, like "What do next, Grog?" We absolutely have to see what's behind this wall. Then we realize our toolbox consists of:
• One old journal
• One cell phone (Pete forgot his)
• Two wallets (only one of which has credit cards in it)
• No tools

So Pete searches around for something, and he comes back from the bathroom with this plumber's wrench. Seriously, like out of a cartoon, this giant plumber's wrench. They must've had a leak or something and left it - whatever. Now it's OURS. So he goes to town on the closet wall, smashing the shit out of it. Meanwhile, somebody next door is screaming "Hey, what the fuck?!" And I'm like "Sorry, it's the headboard, you know how it is, wham-bam, don't worry, we'll be done in a minute!"

The dust finally settles, and there it is – a steel door. Not the size of a regular door. But not like a doggie door either. It's the perfect size for a stooped-over, old inventor who wants to travel to different dimensions.

Holy! Shit! We! Did! It!

We start jumping up and down and hugging like the kids who won the fourth-grade dodgeball tournament (but in total silence, because we don't want the scary-sounding guy next door coming over and ruining our discovery). I calm down and take a look at the door.

The latch. It has a combination lock on it. Four rotating dials, like a big luggage lock. I try it. No go. Damn.

"Okay, Mister Nikola Tesla Expert, what's the combination?"
"Dude. There is NOTHING in this book about a combination. No mention of a lock at all."
"You sure? You read every word? Deciphered any codes? Invisible ink?"
"Really? Invisible ink? Hold on, let me get my wand and cast a spell on it."
"Fuck you."

I shake my head. I can't believe this. Tesla left THIS out of his notes? Didn't leave a combination? Kind of an oversight, don't you think, Nikola? I start frantically flipping through the pages of the journal, then in a pissy rage I toss it across the room. And wouldn't you know it, the back cover fold cracks open and a wee little note pops out.

"That's it!" We rush over and pick it up, hands shaking, waiting for the four digits to pop out and save us. Here's what it reads:

"15 March, 1941: pick up trousers; feed pigeons"

Great. Fucking great. We've unearthed Tesla's really important to-do list from some random day in 1941. Now I'm the one who's ready to pick up and leave, but I stop. I'd like to say I was thinking about you, Julie, and that gave me courage, but really I was just pissed as hell. I'm now on the hook for one demolished hotel room wall, and Pete will NEVER let me forget this moment as long as I live, and I have to go back to my shitty security guard job tomorrow, and I'm never going to do anything awesome.

"No fucking way this lock is beating us. It's like a luggage lock, how hard can it be? Hey Pete, what's the default on a luggage lock, zero-zero-zero-zero, or one-two-three-four?"
"Zeros. I think. I don't know. What am I, Luggage Lock Guy?"

So I go over and turn all the dials to zero. There's no way it could be this ridiculous.
"Whatever, Pete. We gave it a shot, right?"
I try the latch, and this time it turns and the door swings out.

Awesome.

3
Sorry, I Accidentally Hit Send

From: Chip Collins
To: Julie Taylor
Date: June 4, 2015 5:43am
Subject: Sorry, I accidentally hit Send

Julie,

Okay, so where was I at? Oh right...

Awesome.

Wait, first, in case you by some miracle got my previous email and haven't already done so, CALL THE FBI IMMEDIATELY. Here's our last known location:

New Yorker Hotel
481 Eighth Avenue
New York, NY 10001
Room 3327
North Guest Room
Back of Closet
Steel Door (watch your head)
Latch Combination: 0-0-0-0 (really? yes)
Watch your back (you'll find out why in a minute)

Now back to awesome. Well, awesome for a few seconds. After some well-deserved congratulatory hugs (yes, guys can hug), there we stand, chests out, fists on our hips, imaginary capes fluttering in the wind...

Chip Collins and Pete Turner:
Masters of Interdimensional Travel.

So we bound through the door (Pete hits his head – it's hilarious) expecting Hallelujah choruses and chicks waving palm tree branches, maybe a spaceship with a driver waiting for us, holding a silver tray of champagne and strawberries.

Nope. It's a hallway.

And it's not even a nice hallway like in the hotel. It's like a dingy hallway in a warehouse. Gray. Just enough light to let you see how fucking gray it is. And everything's gray. Like, they didn't even paint the trim white or anything, or put yellow and black "Danger! Interdimensional Portal!" signs up. Yawn.

"Wow. What a letdown."
"Yeah. What is this, the help's hallway?"
"The staff."
"The help, the staff, whatever. Is that what this is?"
"I don't know, but it's loooooong."

We start walking (south?), to see how far this hallway goes. See if Tesla's big invention is really just a stupid hallway that leads to the emergency exit. But it turns out it goes on forever. And Julie, I am NOT being figurative, or exaggerating – it goes on FOREVER. We must have walked for a half hour and nothing but hallway as far as you can see in both directions. And doors. Every six feet or so there's a door on both sides. Guess what color?

"Hey, you know what's weird about these doors?"
"They're gray."
"That's not weird, you idiot. There are no numbers."
"Oh yeah."
"Oh shit."
"Oh shit what?"
"Oh shit there are no numbers. How are we going to find the door we came in through?"

We start running like crazy back in the other direction. Of course, Pete's about a thousand yards ahead of me, and I'm wheezing and clutching my chest (I swear, Julie, if you help us get out I'm going to start working out). So I stop, figuring Pete will find the door no problem because I'm pretty sure we left it open.

And then Pete comes running back down the hallway towards me at full speed.

"Holy shit! Holy shit! Holy shit! Holy shit! Holy shit!"

And it's kind of funny, because he sounds like a race car, you know, where his "holy shit"s are faster as he approaches me, and slower when he passes me.

Wait, he's PASSING me? "Pete! What the fu-"

And then something tumbles into me and grabs my leg. Starts dragging me back.

"Pete! Help! It's got me!"

Just when I start crying (Julie, I'm not too proud to say that I cried like I've never cried before), Pete comes back into view, giant plumber's wrench in hand, and whacks the thing in the head. Whack. Dead.

"Dude, I'm sorry. I got scared. I thought you could outrun it."
"You thought I could *outrun* something?! Are you fucking crazy?!"
"Hey, simmer down, I came back for you. I killed that thing. What the fuck is it, a bear? And what the fuck is a bear doing in the help's hallway?"
"It's the STAFF, dude. And I don't think we're in the staff's hallway. And I don't think this is a bear."

I stand up, and me and Pete carefully roll this thing over to get a better look. And that's when shit gets real.

"AHHHHHHH!" "AHHHHHHH!"
(That's both of us screaming.)

Julie, if I'm being really honest, I'm not sure you'll ever see these emails. I might as well be writing them all over the walls with my own poop. So why not tell it like it is, right? No shame, right? Well, we turn this thing over… and I piss my pants. While I'm screaming. While I'm fainting. While Pete is trying to slap me out of it.

It's an alien, Julie. I don't know how the hell an alien got into the hallway, but here it is, dead at our feet. It's got the giant black eyes, like baseball size easily, and the little slits for a nose, and it's smallish, maybe up to my waist. The whole E.T. thing, just like in the movies. But it's furry.

REALLY furry. Like Chewbacca furry, but even more.
Like you'd want to pet it, not smash it in the head with a
plumber's wrench. And after my holy-shit fear wears off (an
eternity, btw), I start to feel a little bad.

"Shit. What if this thing was the last of its kind?"
"Dude. The last of its kind was trying to eat you."
"I don't know. Look how small that mouth is."
"Have you ever seen what a snake does with its mouth?
Swallows a goat whole."
"Right. Good call with the wrench."

So Pete starts heading back, and I follow him. But I can't
help it. I get a pang.
"Are we just gonna leave it?"
"No, you're right. Let's skin it and eat its meat."
"C'mon, Pete. I'm serious."
"What do you want to do, bury it? With what? A plumber's
wrench? I'm leaving."
"Hey, I was just–"

And then it's on me again. The thing.

I scream and try to kick free, but it's no use. I'm in its
clutches. I am going to die. And Pete's laughing. Laughing?

"What the fuck are you laughing at?! Kill it!"
"No. Just let it finish."
"Finish?!"
"He's humping your leg."

Pete's right. This sick little alien is getting off on my leg. So right there in that split second, all my ideas about highly intelligent extraterrestrial beings who spread peace and knowledge throughout the universe go out the window. It's just trying to get some, like the rest of us. (By "rest of us," I'm talking generally, not me specifically. All I'M trying to do is get back home and be good to you, babe. And if I get some? Bonus. Kidding! I'm totally kidding. Not about being good to you. About getting some as a bonus. Whatever, okay I'm a douche.)

So the thing "finishes" – no green alien spooge or anything to contend with, thank God – and Pete starts laughing again. Now we're both laughing, because it's sitting there all satisfied, like if it had a little alien cigarette it would be lighting up right now. And it's just looking at us. Weird – it's actually kind of adorable. The big black eyes, sort of Bambi-like. So I instinctively reach out – Pete's warning me like "remember the goat, dude" – and I pet it. And it's all "ohhh yeahhh" like a cat. (It's not actually talking, God I would've pissed my pants again.)

"So what do you want to name it?"
"Fuck you."
"No I'm serious. Your leg and him are married now, so he should at least have a name."
"How about 'Pete's-an-asshole'?"
"Nice. Nice ring to it. How about 'Indestructo'? He took that wrench like a champ."
"Whatever. I'm sure it has a name or something wherever it came from. Let's just get the hell out of here before we actually do kill something. Or get killed. Later, furry alien dude."

We start walking, and yes, you guessed it, the furry alien dude thing starts following us. Great. We don't need a pet. I can't even keep a plant alive at my apartment. Remember my last pet? Rocky the Ferret. You loved him. But he went bat-shit crazy and started jumping on all the neighbors and we had to put him down. I remember you were crying like Rocky was your own kid. Shit, I was even tearing up a little I guess. Fuck. Now I'm crying again. You know, we could have another pet together someday, it would be awesome. But something that doesn't go bat-shit crazy. And it could sit between us while we're watching TV, and we're both petting it and I accidentally pet your hand. And you're like "what am I, your pet?" And I'm like "I don't know, do you want to be my pet?" And you smile, and you're like "Why don't you be my pet? I'll go get the leash." And then we start laughing our asses off, and the dog (it just became a dog in my imagination) starts barking his head off, wagging his tail, joining in on our big joke, like one big happy family.

Oh boy, time to stop. Woah. Snap out of it, Chip.

So we let the thing follow us, and I'm thinking of the whole pet thing, so I turn around and I'm like "Come here, Bobo." And it scurries up to walk with us. Pete's like "Bobo?" and I'm like "whatever." Then Pete taps one of the doors with his wrench:

"Okay, here's the door."
"Which one? I thought we left it open."
"I thought so too. But this is it."
"How could you possibly know that this is the door? Shouldn't we keep looking for the open one?"

"Chip, I'm pretty good with spatial relations and navigation. If there was an open one a few feet away maybe. But as far as we can see in either direction are closed doors. This is it. Definitely."

"Hmmm."

"Hmmm, what? You want to go home, or you want to stay here with Bobo?"

"Okay. I just have no idea how the hell you know this is the door."

I lean down and look at the latch: 3-4-2-8. I walk over to the next door: 7-7-1-9. Across the hall: 8-0-8-3. WTF?

"Wait. Shouldn't ours be 0-0-0-0?"

"Dude, shit stopped making sense an hour ago. Trust me. Trust me. This is it."

I flip the combination dials to 0-0-0-0 and try the latch. It turns and lets out a little whoosh. Whew! Pete was right. Always trust Pete.

I tell Bobo that he has to get back to wherever he came from (like he understands a word I'm saying – he's actually drooling a little), and we open the door to go home.

It's not the hotel closet.

I don't know if there's an opposite to a hotel closet, but this is it. It's like a forest, but all the trees are blue – if you can even call them trees. And before I can even try to comprehend what we're seeing, some metal thing whizzes past my ear and lodges into the wall behind me. So of course I start screaming, and Bobo runs away down the infinite hallway, and Pete lunges at the door, slams it shut, and turns the latch.

"Oops. Maybe it's the next one."

I jump on Pete (still screaming), and we fight like some sad amateur professional wrestlers, gouging each others eyes and pulling hair, you know, really classy. Once we're tuckered out (well, I'm tuckered out and Pete's just tired of kicking my ass), the strangest thing happens – I start an inventory of the shit that is about to go wrong:

1. Pete's credit card will be charged for room damages, something he'll remind me of every five minutes for the rest of our lives.

2. My car is in the garage (again), and Ed's going to be a total dick about it if I come late to pick it up (again).

3. I think I left Pete's stereo on when we swung by his place, so his neighbors are going to complain – and that's the third time, so he might be looking for a new apartment. (He doesn't know about that one yet, so don't tell him when you rescue us.)

4. My mom brought over a pan of lasagna, which is on the fridge (not IN the fridge – I know, I'm a schmuck). That is going to be RIPE.

Before I can complete my list of disasters (which will never end until you rescue us pretty please), Pete picks me up, makes sure my ear isn't bleeding, and turns into Mister Action Man.

"I'll try the next one. Stand back."
"Uh, you think?"

He chooses the door to the left of the really dangerous blue forest with hailing weapons, flips the combination dials to 0-0-0-0 and tries the latch. It turns and lets out the little whoosh, just like the last one.

> (Official Interdimensional Travel Observation #1: Apparently the universal combination for an Interdimensional Portal is 0-0-0-0. Pretty awe-inspiring, right? Also, it looks like once a portal door closes, it automatically resets to a random four-digit combination. Just to totally mess with you.)

Pete grabs his plumber's wrench. I grab the metal thing out of the wall. (Bobo grabs nothing, because he's completely gone.) We're both cringing, waiting for a T-rex to pop out and eat us or something. Then Pete cracks open the door just a wee bit.

IT'S THE HOTEL ROOM!

Oh my God. We're saved! I immediately promise the following:
- No more of this dimension traveling shit.
- I'm going to work out.
- I'm going to get a real job. (Not with the FBI, no offense guys!)
- I'm going to marry you. Whoops. Yes, I just said that. And you know what? It felt good. Yes. You will be my bride. We will ride astride white horses down a pristine beach during sunset, reciting our vows to the seagulls, laughing and splashing in the sea. Definitely.

Pete goes through first (not hitting his head this time), and
I follow (yes, hitting my head, and Pete laughs at me). And
I don't know if it's just that "holy-shit-I-got-my-life-back"
feeling, but the room looks fine. Shove the ironing board
and robes back into the closet, close the door, and it's good
as new. Boom. Awesome.

We head downstairs, with a skip in our step. Yes, we're The
Masters of Interdimensional Travel, thank you very much.
Then we take care of the essentials:
- Put the lasagna IN the fridge.
- Turn Pete's stereo off.
- Go out for a celebration beer.

We hit Harper's Tavern (you know, where we first spilled
beer on each other and I was pawing you to help you clean
it but really copping a pretty nice feel) and I remember:
"Wait! I have to call Julie!" But guess what? My phone is
dead, and Pete's is still at his place. Luckily, there's a CVS
right next to the bar, so I pick up a charger (yes, another
charger, to add to my collection of three hundred or so, and
yes, I made Pete pay for it).

We get back to the bar, and I'm waiting for my phone to
have enough juice to call you, enjoying a Blue Moon, feeling
like King-of-the-Universe-About-to-Call-His-Queen, and
this cop walks in. No big deal, right?

He walks over to the bartender, who points down to us.
So the cop comes over to us, no introductions, and grabs
my left hand and Pete's left hand.

"Where are your bands?"

And we're both like "Bands?"

"Don't play idiot, retards."

"Hey, isn't that a little–"

Instantly, me and Pete are bent over a table, zip-cuffed, sipping our own spilled beer through our noses. Then the cop starts the crazy talk into his radio:

"Base, I've got two Untrackables. And they're not on the Watch List. Yeah, likely they're terrorists. I'll bring them in for booking and waterboarding, Get the tank ready."

What the? Bands? Untrackables? Waterboarding? TANK?

Then it hits me: this is NOT home.

4
I Met Myself,
and I Am Actually
Not Bad Looking

From: Chip Collins
To: Julie Taylor
Date: June 4, 2015 5:43am
I met myself, and I am actually not bad looking

Hi Julie,

Okay, so obviously we lived through the Evil-Cop-from-a-dimension-strikingly-similar-to-our-own episode, because I'm writing this to you. I just had to give my poor fingers a break (you know how hard it is to type a thirty-page email on a four-inch screen?) and charge my phone.

> IMPORTANT NOTE: If you're reading this, I'm assuming it's because you're waiting for the FBI to come over and make their way over here to the Strange-O-Matic machine and get us the hell out of here. If for some reason you still haven't called, PLEASE DO SO IMMEDIATELY. Pretty please. You're the best, babe. XOXO.

So how do we escape the Evil Cop? You are NOT going to believe it. He's walking us out of the bar so he can spend the next few hours torturing us, and (this is the part you are not going to believe):

We literally bump into ourselves.

Alternate Me and Alternate Pete – I assume out for a congratulatory beer after finding their dimension's copy of the Interdimensional Transfer Apparatus, and pretty oblivious to the outside world – bump right into us.

I know me and Pete (and our identical counterparts) should explode from the paradox, or at least dissolve into blubbering insanity, but this is the only thought that pops into my head:

Hey, I'm not a bad-looking guy.

Obviously Pete's thinking the same thing, because the two Pete's are smiling at each other. So there we are, Chip and Pete, and Alternate Chip and Alternate Pete. Same faces, same hair, same clothes. Same everything. All smiling like idiots at each other.

> (Official Interdimensional Travel Observation #2: you'd think that meeting yourself in another dimension would cause a total freak-out of the infinite order, pants-pissing, screaming, etc. But it's the total opposite: weirdly calming. Like "Hey bro, I know you! Let's go get a beer.")

But the whole love-fest is immediately cut short by Evil Cop, who does a few triple-takes (kind of comical, just not at the moment), then shoves all four of us up against his car. He checks the other Chip and Pete, and sure enough, they've got bands around their left wrists. So Evil Cop scans their bands with the register scanner thing he got from The Gap.

"Okay, retards. You two are clean. But if you can't explain why I'm looking at both of your identical twins – who DON'T have bands – you're ALL going to the tank."

We're standing there, bellies up against the squad car, frantically searching for some weak story to hold on to. And I can tell poor Alternate Me is dying to ask us a million questions. But Evil Cop's not waiting.

"NOW."

And then Alternate Me (my hero) comes up with this gem: "Sir, ah, sorry for the confusion. They're our, ah, robots."

Robots? I don't know whether to laugh or release my bowels.

"Robots. Really. Don't lie to me, punk."
Then Alternate Pete chimes in.
"Uh, yes officer. We work at the, uh, Columbia University Advanced Robotics Lab, and this was part of an experiment. To see how people interact with very realistic robots."
"So you want me to believe these two are robots."
"Yes. Very realistic robots."
"Bullshit, punk. Prove it."

At this point, I'm preparing myself for whatever "the tank" is, and I can't tell if Pete is more afraid, or more pissed at me, because he's grinding his teeth again and glaring at me. Meanwhile, Alternate Me doubles down on the robot story (just like I knew he would. Man, he's awesome – I know, I know, when he's not being a douche):

"Sure thing, officer. Robot Chip, power down."

Hmm. Power down. How do very realistic robots power down? Do I bend over and do that arm swing thing like the dance? Do I just freeze? Do I make bleep noises and go through some kind of shutdown sequence? Do I –

"Power down NOW, Robot Chip."

Whoops. Got it. I just relax everything and let my body fall to the pavement (which hurts like a motherfucker, btw). I'm not sure if Evil Cop buys it, but he lets out a snort, which sounds promising.

"Now make him get up."
"Okay. Robot Chip, power on and get up."

As I "power up," I notice we're attracting a bit of a crowd. Man, New Yorkers love this shit. Doesn't matter what dimension you're in. iPhones are coming out, people are taking pictures. The meat-on-a-stick guy on the corner is pitching the crowd like a cotton candy vendor at a circus. Boy, we're definitely creating ripples in the Interdimensional Continuum with this little show. Heck, you might even see me on Instagram. (Maybe not YOU you, but Alternate You, who I'm sure is awesome, too. But not as awesome as you.)

"Okay. Now show me his wiring, or control panel, or something."

Uh-oh. I can tell Alternate Me is at a total loss. I know that blank look. I know it very well. Evil Cop is definitely playing us, knows we don't have shit. Then I feel the metal thingy in my back pocket. Hmm. Nothing to lose, right? So I finally speak up (in my lovable, ever-so-subtle robot voice): "Master Chip. You forgot my remote when you sent us to the bar." I'm zipcuffed though, so I can barely get the thing out of my pocket. But Evil Cop spots the shiny object (yes, I'm getting the sense that even though he's a tool, he's not the sharpest one) and he grabs it from me.

"Give me that, punk. Huh. Cool."

And I gotta say – if somebody gave this to you and told you it was a remote instead of a weapon, you'd believe it. It actually sort of looks like one. The tip is like an arrow shape, but the rest is a thin metal tube with recessed buttons down one side. Like a totally badass looking remote. I'm pretty sure I even hear some "Ooooh"s from the crowd.

So Evil Cop, who never stops to ask for directions, or reads an instruction manual, never looks both ways before crossing the street, or uses caution in anything he's ever done, points it at me.

"What's this button do?" He presses the top button. Nothing. So he shakes it and taps the tip against his other hand.

And he freezes instantly.

Wow.

We're all afraid to move. Is he kidding? Is this some sick Evil Cop trick where we try to escape and he shoots us all in the back? Is the thing going to explode in his hands? But after a few seconds he's still not moving. Not blinking. Not exploding. Nothing.

> (Official Interdimensional Travel Observation #3: Be VERY careful with stuff you pick up in other dimensions. There are infinite possibilities, and infinite ways to accidentally kill yourself.)

So the four of us are standing there, waiting. And then I notice that the growing crowd around us is waiting, too. (It's the kind of crowd that you know is hoping for an explosion.)

Alternate Me breaks the silence and starts clapping. "Okay folks, show's over! Give these actors a hand! These UNDERPAID actors! Pete, pass around the hat!" What a genius – want to disperse a crowd in New York City? Go around and ask for money. I love that guy. So Alternate Pete walks around with his hand out and everyone stops clapping and starts fleeing like he's got leprosy. Perfect.

Next, once we're pretty much alone, we move in silent and perfect unison, like the U.S. Bobsled Team:

Step 1. Alternate Chip and Pete drag Evil Cop into his car.

Step 2. We slip into the back seat.

Step 3. Alternate Chip finds a little knife in the cop's belt and cuts the zipcuffs off our wrists.

Step 4. I DELICATELY remove the metal thingy (I need a better name for that) from Evil Cop's hand.

Step 5. Alternate Pete gets on the radio, doing his best Evil Cop impression: "Base, we're good. False alarm. Retards were clean. I'll check in at eleven."

Step 6. We close all the doors.

Let the million questions begin. I'm not sure if it matters, but I figured you might want to know who's saying what:

Alternate Me: "Hey guys, let me guess. You came from the INTERDIMENSIONAL TRANSFER APPARATUS."

Me: "Yeah. What an annoying name."

Alternate Me: "I know, right?"

Me: "Totally. And the all caps thing."

Alternate Me: "So what happened?"

Me: "We went in, and tried to come back. We thought this was home. But I'm guessing it's another dimension, mostly like ours."

Pete: "Except for the bands. What the fuck is up with that?"

Alternate Pete: "Bands. To track you. Permanent fixture. Some stupid asshole came up with that after World War Three. You don't have them in your dimension?"

Me and Pete: "World War Three?!"

Alternate Me: "World War Three. So what."

Me: "There was no World War Three!"

Alternate Me: "Don't tell me there was no World War Three. My mother served two tours."

Me: "Holy shit! Mom served in a war? Did she survive?"

Alternate Me: "Of course, dude. She's awesome. She even made me a lasagna tonight."

Me: "Oh right. Hey, I put it in the fridge for you, by the way."

Alternate Me: "Whoops. Thanks."

Pete: "God, I thought listening to ONE of you was a pain in the ass. Can we get the hell out of here before another cop shows up?"

Pete, as usual, is right. I hit the Dunkin' Donuts across the street, and we set up Frozen Evil Cop with a dozen, and stick a chocolate glazed in his hand. Good enough. Then we scram on foot and grab a cab back to the New Yorker Hotel. (Side note: Alternate Me makes Alternate Pete pay for the cab – it's priceless.)

We walk up to the room in shifts so we don't cause another scene (us Masters of Interdimensional Travel know what we're doing), and meet at the closet. We order room service and bullshit for a little while, comparing notes. Meanwhile I'm wondering why our alternates are even here. Shouldn't they be stuck in another part of the hallway? Or another dimension? They broke down the wall but didn't go through the door?

"So you guys didn't go through the door?"
"Nope. We got as far as the door, but we didn't go in."

They stayed put. Man, these guys are smart. Smarter than us.

"…because we couldn't figure out the latch combination."

Or maybe not.

For whatever reason – maybe the wristbands screw with your common sense – these guys couldn't get 0-0-0-0. Duh. Points off, Alternate Me. But I still love him, so I go into protective-older-brother mode:

"Well, that's a good thing, because you can never go in."
"Wait. You're not going to tell us the combination?"
"Dude. What do you think? Did you not just see how crazy shit got when we visited your dimension?"
"Right. So you guys get to have all the fun."
"You call this fun?"

Alternate Chip knows I'm right. He's got that look of true understanding. (Yes, believe it or not I sometimes have the look of true understanding, babe.) So we agree that they're going to patch up the wall and destroy their copy of the journal, and we say our goodbyes. Then Pete and I step through the ITA (I refuse to type INTERDIMENSIONAL TRANSFER APPARATUS one more time). But something stops me. I stand halfway through the doorway and call Alternate Me over.

"Hey, Chip, do you remember that time Julie came over, and she was joking about wedding dresses, how ugly they all were?"
"Sure."
"Well, she's full of shit. It's her dream. She wants to marry you. And she's perfect for you. She laughs at the same movies as you. She cries when she sees those abandoned dog commercials on TV. She eats your chili and says she likes it even tough it's terrible. She made you a telephone out of two coffee cups and a string. And her smile is like… it's like the sun. It's warm and it's bright, and there's nothing that can hide from it. And she listens to you, dude. I mean, who does that? So you go right now and apologize for being a douche for the past two months. And you make it right. And you ask her to marry you. Do you hear me?"

He thinks about it for a second. He nods. And what a sap, he's got a little tear running down his cheek. But I do too, so who's the sap?

Julie, I know there's a pretty good possibility I may never see you again, but I made it right. At least for one of an infinite number of Chips.

That lucky bastard.

5
Lists Make Me
Feel Better

From: Chip Collins
To: Julie Taylor
Date: June 4, 2015 5:43am
Lists make me feel better

Hi Julie,

I know you love my lists. I think this one is your current favorite:

Top Ten Things I Love About Chinese Food:

1. The names are funny (Cream of Sum Yung Gai).

2. It's delicious.

3. It doesn't try to pretend it's good for you.

4. It doesn't matter if you over-order. After a couple of hours, you're hungry enough to go back and finish the sesame chicken. And the lo mein. And the boneless spare ribs, etc.

5. I can almost always get someone else to pay for it (Pete, you, my Mom, Ted, the options are pretty limitless).

6. All movies are better with chinese food.

7. Wong's is literally right downstairs from my apartment. I can smell it from my bedroom.

8. It's the breakfast of champions.

9. Free wine (only on dine-in orders, max of two glasses)

10. Head-scratching fortunes ("Trees grow high, but never reach the sky." Huh? What a downer!)

So, since I have nothing but time at the moment (I've already written you three "Please Save Us" emails, I think that's enough for now), and there's nothing in this infinite hallway that's interesting to look at, and I am DEFINITELY NOT opening up another one of these doors until I figure out what the fuck is going on, I'm going to write you some lists.

Things I Did This Week:

1. Started a shitty job as a security guard.

2. Discovered the lost journal of Nikola Tesla.

3. Pete punched me in the face.

4. Destroyed a hotel wall with a plumber's wrench.

5. Entered a (very gray) interdimensional hallway.

6. Almost killed, then befriended, a furry alien.

7. Met a version of myself from another dimension. (Who was not bad looking, btw)

8. Escaped from an Evil Cop using a metal weapon taken from a dimension filled with blue trees. (I'm laughing. How can you type that without laughing?)

9. Realized I love you. (It's okay if you shed a tear here)

10. Somehow avoided death.

Wow. Pretty bitchin week, right? I'm actually kind of proud of myself. Although I'm pretty sure Pete's not proud of me. In fact, I've compiled Pete's top comments today.

Pete's Top Six Comments to Me Today:

1. "Fuck you."

2. "What are you, an idiot?"

3. "Really? Really?"

4. "Well, here we are, 'reposing' in the hallway they'll find our dead bodies in. Thanks, dude."

5. "Shhh! What the fuck was that?"

6. "Hey, are you writing these down?"

He sort of smiles when he says that last one, though, so I think we're still okay. And we kind of have to be, right? This is it. Just me and Pete. Pete and me. Just the two of us.

And Bobo!

He's back! The man with the plan! (I know, that doesn't make any sense, but I'm happy to see him). I swear if he had a tail he'd be wagging it like crazy. He runs over (and yes, humps my leg again), and it's like a puppy rescue or something. Even Pete is smiling and petting him. Wow. Okay. Energy's a little higher, we're all happy for the moment. So we decide (not Bobo, I'm not so sure about his decision-making skills) to take stock, get our extreme survival mojo going. First – what are our resources?

Chip and Pete's Current Resources:

1. Bobo (does he count as a resource?)

2. One really big plumber's wrench

3. One metal weapon thingy (you know what? I'm going to call it the *Shogun*. Like some insane futuristic samurai weapon. Cool, right? "Hand me the *Shogun*, Luke.")

4. One old journal

5. One cell phone

6. One cell phone charger from CVS

7. Three wallets (we stole Alternate Pete's for some extra cash in case we need it down the road. And don't judge me. Those guys will be fine. They're better off than us.)

We think we've got Bobo figured out – as in *not-much-to-figure-out* – so the only thing on our list that's a question mark is the Shogun. (Pete digs the name, so we're sticking with it.) Based on its shape, how we've seen it used (flung at my face from another dimension), and what happened with Evil Cop (he pressed a button and then touched the tip), we put together this:

Official Shogun Quick Start Guide:

Step 1. Press desired button.

Step 2. Fling at enemy.

Step 3. When tip touches enemy, they will _____.

We already know what button number one does: freeze. (Not freeze like cold, freeze like freeze-dance. Like "FREEZE, PUNK!" I know, you get it). But what do the other buttons do? How do we test it? I sure as hell am not risking my life. And Pete's looking at me, and dammit, I know exactly what he's thinking:

Bobo.

"Come on, he's indestructible. That wrench literally would've killed your average bear."
"Dude, come on, he doesn't deserve this."
"Chip. I popped Bobo with everything I had, and look at

him. What's he doing right now?"

"He's licking your hand."

"He loves me. And I tried to kill him."

"Yeah, but you know the last time I trusted your instincts I got a Shogun flung at me."

"Fine. You got a better idea?"

And actually, I don't. I'm too busy making lists, trying to maintain enough control so the next time something weird happens (a virtual guarantee) I don't piss my pants again. So I agree and we test all the buttons on Bobo. Being the pseudo-scientists we are, we of course repeat the first button to see if it has the same effect. Yup. Frozen solid. Bobo-sickle. For like a half an hour. We get so bored waiting at one point we play Bobo Curling. (His fur is really almost frictionless, and the floor of the hallway is pretty smooth, so of course Pete wins by like four hundred yards, and of course we play loser-drags-Bobo's-body-to-the-starting-line, so now of course my back hurts.)

Anyway, we now have the Shogun, a weapon capable of some pretty cool shit.

Pretty Cool Shit the Shogun Can Do:

Button 1: Freeze.

Button 2: Electrocute.

Button 3: Stun with sound wave blast. (Our ears are still ringing. Holy cow, if you ever want to wake the neighbors a mile away this is perfect.)

Button 4: Some kind of field, like force bubble or something. It traps you. Let's go with "Field Trap."

Button 5: Nothing. (Maybe you only get a certain number of rounds? Maybe we got a bad unit?)

And there's Bobo, after all this, still licking Pete's hand. I'm trying not to think Bobo's a masochist, but Pete's the one dishing out the punishment, and he's the one getting his hand licked. And yeah, I'm a little jealous. I'll admit it.

Okay, so we've got our resources. What's next? The lay of the land. Let's get a really good look at this hallway, and see what we're dealing with.

Things to Know About the INTERDIMENSIONAL TRANSFER APPARATUS (ITA):

1. It's gray. Grayer than any gray you've ever seen.

2. Every six feet is a door on both sides of the hallway. Also gray.

3. Each door has a latch (guess what color) with a 4-digit luggage lock that automatically resets to a random number when you close it. Nice touch.

4. The Universal Combination is 0-0-0-0 (I know, hard to commit to memory, but try)

5. There are power outlets. Yes, believe it or not, Tesla designed this whatever-it-is with regular power outlets every twenty feet, like he thought the help – the STAFF! – might need to come in once in a while and vacuum. So now I can charge my phone, and if we had a toaster oven, we could heat up our pizza. If we had pizza.

6. The lighting is weird. Well, I mean, EVERYTHING is weird, but we can't figure out the lighting. There are no fixtures and no shadows, so you can't really place where

it's coming from. It's just there. The good news (yes, this is what I'm considering good news these days) is that it's on the warm side, not like fluorescent lights. It's like a glow sort of. A warm, dim glow. Hey, I've never written about light before – I feel like an interior designer: "Let's put the dim glow in the corner. No, let's put it EVERYWHERE. It'll be fabulous."

7. The hallway is infinite. Self-explanatory. Tesla must have designed how it would look, but he couldn't have built it. It's infinite. (Have I mentioned it's infinite?)

8. The different dimensions behind the doors are not totally random. Almost, but not quite. Here's how we figure it out (Yes! I get to do a SUB-list.):

A) We put Bobo in front of the doors.

B) We open the doors and wait for Bobo to be attacked, or sucked into a vortex, or killed.

C) When we get the all clear, me and Pete check out the view. And let me tell you, you expect these dimensions to be similar, right? WRONG. One door will lead to a room full of 10-foot-tall orange guys playing craps ("Sorry boys, get back to what you were doing"), and the next will be the frigid vacuum of space (we close the door quick on those before Bobo gets sucked out). And we start to see how infinite the possibilities are. Like for that vacuum of space one: maybe in that dimension the Earth didn't quite form right, or maybe it got destroyed by an asteroid that happened to be one degree off its course a million years ago. And there we are opening up a doorway to the exact spot in the universe where the hotel room should be. But there never was a hotel room. Or a Hotel New Yorker. Or New York City. Or Earth.

BUT...

Every ten or so, we open a door to sheetrock – the inside wall of the hotel closet. Not the same dimension, obviously, but close. Like Tesla got through the ITA, and the hotel covered it up, but somewhere along the line me and Pete never got there. Maybe I never found the journal. Or maybe Pete talked me out of it. Or maybe I got into college and actually did something with my life, so I didn't have to go get that shitty security guard job in the first place. Again, infinite possibilities.

It goes on like that, every ten or so doors are the hotel room. So it's not totally random. But we haven't hit another one where the closet wall is down and we can see into the room. Why? Are we the ONLY Chip and Pete that have figured this out? The ONLY ones to get this far? The ONLY ones that know the default combination on a luggage lock? Wow, we're pretty awesome, huh? So I'm standing there feeling like the Smartest Chip across all dimensions, and Pete interrupts my special moment.

"Hey. Snap out of it. Check this out."

It's another hotel room with the wall down. But this time we're not jumping up and down. We're learning fast that this could be home, but it could also be the lair of Evil Cop Two.

We backtrack to the last dimension we actually entered (where we met Alternate Me and Alternate Pete). BTW, for reference, we've been scratching numbers and notes on each of the doors as we go:

Door #1: Evil Cop (but Chip and Pete are cool)
Door #2: Dangerous Blue Forest
Door #3: 10-Foot Tall Orange Guys Playing Craps
Door #4: Frigid Vacuum of Space DO NOT OPEN… etc…

Door #83. That's the next one with the wall down.
Mathematicians that we are, we guess that every 83 doors
or so might be our ticket home. 83. Our new lucky number.
Not as funny as 69 would have been, or as clean as 100, but
it's better than a million, so it'll do.

We step into the doorway, and Bobo starts tugging at Pete's
pants leg. He won't let go.

"Bobo. What the fuck? Down, boy."
"Ha. Who's married now?"
"Fuck you."

Pete pries himself loose and gives Bobo this really stern
look.

"Now listen, Bobo, I don't know if you can understand me.
But me and Chip have to see if this is our home. We need to
get home. Don't you want to find your home?"

Bobo just stands there staring at Pete with those giant
Bambi eyes. Blink. Blink. Pete's tough-guy act is falling
apart.

"Okay, listen, I promise. No matter what, we'll either
bring you with us, or we'll help you find your home, too. I
promise. Got it?"

Blink. Blink.

"Shit. Whatever. Just stay here until we get back."

We step through into the hallway, and we're immediately assaulted. By a smell. What the fuck is that SMELL? It's like a thousand acres of horse shit with a thousand gallons of Eau de French Whore poured on top. Peee-eeww. I'm thinking it's Pete.

"Dude. Did you fart?"
"Fart? Are you serious? Dude, that's an insult even to your grandma's farts."
"Hey. That's my grandma you're talking about."
"Yeah. And her farts were like a nuclear blast over a city built out of manure. And this is worse."
"Wait. You remember my grandmother's farts? She's been dead for like ten years."
"Dude. They're burned into my olfactory memory. I will never forget. But like I said, this is worse. So can we get the fuck going?"

We're both gagging, so we bury our noses into our elbows and make our way downstairs to scope out whether this is home or not. But that smell is NOT going away. Man, is somebody's grandma walking around all the hallways farting?

We walk over to the concierge desk, and the girl has her back to us, oblivious to not only us but the stench. How? So I tap the little bell thingy and Pete asks:

"Excuse me, what is that SMELL?"

The girl turns around, and we both yelp. Julie, it's not that she's ugly. It's worse. She is literally covered with these sores and pustules, head to toe. Purples, reds, oranges, greens – the most disgusting rainbow of skin color I've ever seen. And I can literally see the stench rising off her. Yikes. I'm practically throwing up in my mouth.

"Uh, Gentlemen. Are you all right? Your skin… it's… deformed. And I believe the smell may be you, I'm sorry to say it's foul. Do you need me to call a doctor?"

OUR skin? OUR smell? WE'RE foul? This girl is crazy. And then the manager walks over and the crazy really starts.

"Miss Barber, is there a prob- OH MY DEAR LORD. Sirs, I'm embarrassed to ask, but may I help? You've obviously been horribly disfigured by some disease, and your… aroma. Something needs to be done."

Me and Pete give each other *the look*: MUST GET BACK. DIMENSION #83 IS NOT HOME.

I pull my elbow down to respond to the guy, and a full blast of his stench hits me. So instead of saying something smart, I puke right on his suit. Pete actually laughs.

"Holy shit. You just did that."
"Yeah, I know I did that. Thanks."

He turns to the manager. "We're sorry, sir. Obviously my friend here is sick. I'm going to get him back up to the room, and if you could call a doctor that would be great."

I reach out to help blot some of my vomit off the poor guy (even though it helped him smell better if you ask me), and Pete grabs me, and pulls me down the hallway.

"Fuck. Back to the ITA."

Pete's pissed. Another no-go. Dimension #83 is bullshit. I'm sniffing back tears, and he's had enough. At the top of the stairs, he grabs my shoulders and shakes me.

"Listen, Chip. Stop crying. Stop. I know you're a baby, so there's only so much you can handle. But you have to keep trusting me. We have to keep moving forward. We'll figure this out. And fuck, if we don't… at least we have each other."

Holy shit. Pete is NOT a man of heartfelt moments. I can't help it. I lunge at him and hug him and I just stand like that until he ruins the moment.

"Get off me. Now."

Whoops. Almost forgot we're in the middle of a list. What number were we at, 9? Okay…

The Ninth Thing to Know Ab out the INTERDIMENSIONAL TRANSFER APPARATUS (ITA):
9. Here's the biggee. Drum roll, please. Now right before we come back through the ITA, I notice the clock on the hotel room dresser – 10:04pm. And it hits me. That's about the same time it said when we left Alternate Chip and Pete back in dimension number one – SEVERAL HOURS AGO.

Hmmm. To test the theory that's developing in my neanderthal brain, we wait maybe ten minutes, then peek back into dimension #83 (holding our noses this time) to see what time the clock says.

10:04pm.

No time difference. Okay. Second part of the theory. We walk into dimension #83 and stand there for five minutes, right next to the dresser, in the insane stench, to see what the clock says.

10:09pm.

Five minutes have passed. Okay. We're inside a dimension and time passes normally. We try the whole thing again, same result.

Okay. Third part of my theory. I look through the emails I've sent you, and yup – they're all stamped with the same time. So here's the Number Nine Thing to Know:

**Time does not pass when you're
between dimensions in the ITA.**

At first, this seems like good news. Hey, at least we won't grow old trying to find our way out, right? We've got nothing but time! We can take all the time in the world, and when we get back, it'll be June 4, 2015 5:43am. And we won't have aged a day. We've got forever!

Wait.

We've got FOREVER.

We're in a hallway that never ends, with doors to infinity. We've got eternal time to roam around like idiots. We will never grow old. Never die. And possibly never find the right doorway. I mean, what are the chances we open the right one out of ALL OF THEM? There IS NO all of them! And I think an email's going to get to you? TIME doesn't even work in here! We're going to be stuck in this goddam hallway FOREVER, looking for home. FOREVER.

FOREVER.

My crying this time isn't the cry of fear, or disappointment. It's the little whimpers of a guy without hope.

Hopelessness.

God, what a shitty feeling.

This whole crazy time, I guess I just assumed somehow we'd be okay, that the puzzle would somehow work itself out. That's how my whole life's been. (And usually it's someone like you or Pete bailing me out, thank you, btw.) But now I know my free ride is over. Karma has finally caught up with me in a BIG way, holding out his hand for payment: "Hey Chip, guess what? You're going to have to pay for your own goddam chinese food from now on."

Ugh. I'm trapped in between dimensions with my best friend, a furry alien, an infinite choice of doors, and no hope. It's over. Shit.

And the worst part? I'll never feel your face in my hands again. We'll never rent *Evil Dead 2* again. I'll never put another band-aid on your finger after you cut it chopping tomatoes and you're crying even though it's really nothing. I'll never get to watch you walk down the aisle in the wedding dress you insist is ugly but secretly love. I'll never hear your sense of humor in our son Dale (we have two kids in my imagination) or see your beautiful red hair on our daughter Gail (wait, rhyming names? probably not.) We'll never walk our grandkids down Main Street at DisneyWorld. We'll never sit there at the end, all gray and worn-down, and chuckle about all the stupid shit we've done over the years, and all the love we made.

I have a jillion choices I can make, a jillion doors, but I can't have the thing I really choose: you.

Goodbye, babe.

6
Forget That
Last Part

From: Chip Collins
To: Julie Taylor
Date: June 4, 2015 5:43am
Forget that last part

Julie!

Yes, It's me – back from the brink! Man, I thought that was my last email. Hope was gone. I was ready to turn the Shogun on myself (although that would be a cool way to go, very samurai-like, right?). And then it happened...

Scratch.

Scratch.

Scratch. Scratch. Scratch.

Scratch. Scratch. Scratch. Scratch. Scratch. Scratch. Scratch. Scratch. Scratch. Scratch. Scratch. Scratch. Scratch. Scratch. Scratch. Scratch. Scratch. Scratch.

"Dude, stop scratching!"
"Dude, don't look at me. It's Bobo."

But it's not Bobo. Bobo's just sitting there. And man he can sit. Like, you have to poke him sometimes to make sure he's alive. So no, it's definitely not him. I jerk my head around like a… what's good at hearing? A meerkat? So I'm jerking my head around like a meerkat, looking for the source of this annoying scratching sound. It's barely there, but it's annoying as shit. Even when you've given up on life, annoying sounds are annoying sounds and must be dealt with.

It's the journal. There are scratching sounds coming from the journal.

Pete looks at it. I look at it. (Bobo looks at his feet and wiggles his toes.) I open the journal right to the last page with writing on it and I can't believe what I'm seeing. Somebody's writing in the journal. No, not somebody.

Nikola Tesla's writing in the journal!

Wait. How the hell is Tesla writing in the journal? He was around 86 when he walked into the ITA. So he's long dead by– NO. When he walked in (or tripped in, considering how small he made these doors), time stopped. So he could TOTALLY be alive. 86 and half-baked, but alive. And maybe, just maybe…

The journal starts filling up with entries, so fast I can't keep up. So I flip right to the back page and wait for them to arrive. The scratching stops somewhere in the middle, so I flip to that page. And Julie, for your reading enjoyment, I'm typing out the whole thing for you:

> "7 January, 1943: I, Nikola Tesla, inventor of the INTERDIMENSIONAL TRANSFER APPARATUS, *(Wow, after 70 years, he really can't get enough of saying that)* have reached an end to my adventures. A conclusion to perhaps the greatest exploration in Universal History, the story of which is contained in these treasured pages. I wish to return to dimension #234,698,594,394,683 and share these wonders with my fellow man."

Holy cow – Tesla is not only alive, but he knows EXACTLY which dimension we belong in, and he's coming this way!

WE'RE GOING HOME!

I start my Oscar speech, thanking everyone I've ever known, on my knees weeping with joy. Pete starts dancing around with Bobo (btw, that Bobo can dance!), and we're all pretty giddy. We're going home! And Tesla left a cute P.S., too. I can't wait to read it to Pete:

> "P.S. There is one slight complication. I am being held captive in an interdimensional prison of quite an advanced nature. It may be several millennia before I can devise an escape."

Pete stops dancing and looks at me. Bobo keeps dancing, totally unaware that the Ultimate Rug has been pulled out from under us. We're dead. Again. I drop the journal. Thank God Pete's got one last joke in him.

"Tesla, that nut. What's he gotten himself mixed up in this time?"

And I laugh. You know, that laugh like it's the end of your life and you just can't give a fuck anymore. And Pete starts laughing. We're howling, Julie. I swear, I'm not kidding when I say I've never laughed like that. We're both on our asses now, crying from laughter, and I'm grabbing my side because it hurts, and Bobo is just standing there (he finally stopped dancing), blinking, looking at us like he knows we've reached the end. And I wonder to myself: does Bobo know it's the end for him, too?

Well, that thought sobers me up for a second, enough to roll onto my side and curl up to ease the pain in my gut. And the journal is right there, an inch from my face, and I see it.

"Hey dude, wait. There's more."

> "P.P.S. There may be another way. Although the journal I left behind clearly has been mishandled, and no brave adventurer has joined me on my journeys, perchance some smart fellow might happen upon it in the next few hundred years and recognize its worth. Then it may be possible to communicate between the journals. I could conceivably lead him to this godforsaken and dangerous place, enlist his aid in a daring rescue, then as cohorts travel home for a shot of whiskey and a lengthy retelling of my tales of wonderment."

Pete's frowning. "Great choice. Try our luck here, or face near-certain death to save Tesla."
"Yeah, but he can get us HOME, dude."

The word "home" rings in both our ears, and Pete nods at me like General Eisenhower giving the go-ahead to invade Normandy (remind me to fact-check that later). I grab my pen (I took it from the hotel, it was shiny) and scrawl my first words to Tesla, hoping like hell the journal works both ways:

"Okay, Tesla. Where to?"

In that moment, I realize that I've already changed. I've been to the bottom, so there is nowhere to go but up. I've shed my skin and survived the first trials. And I'm certain of something, maybe for the first time in my life. I KNOW. I know that even if you can't come and save us, I'm coming back. Coming back to reclaim my damn life. Coming back to make it up to Pete. Coming back to be with you.

There is a way back. And I'm coming home.

Part Two
Where the Hell is Tesla?

7
Being a Superhero?
Turns Out It Sucks.

From: Chip Collins
To: Julie Taylor
Date: June 4, 2015 5:43am
Being a superhero? Turns out it sucks.

Hi Julie,

So me and Pete are standing there on 86th, helping the good citizens of New York City up from the flooded subway station. They're hugging us, thanking us through their tears. Cops are following our instructions, getting people to safety. Firetrucks are barreling down Broadway, sirens blaring. And I'm thinking:

Oh yeah. Being a superhero *rocks*.

Suddenly there's a rumble. Like an earthquake, but… alive. Then silence. All the sirens stop. You can hear a pin drop. Everybody (I'm talking a crowd of thousands) is frozen still, looking at us for some kind of answer. But before we can say a word, the street buckles right in the middle and gives way, leaving this giant 50-foot diameter hole in the ground.
"Uh, dude. This is not good."
Pete inches toward the edge and peeks down.
"Calm down. There's nothing down ther-"

Instantly a giant thing (sea monster? dinosaur? Satan himself?) explodes out of the hole, hurling taxis and concrete everywhere, and landing with a watery thud right in front of us. Julie, this thing is HUGE. Like full city block huge. Shaped like a big slug, but with little t-rex arms, and a big horn on his head. So it lifts this crazy-ass ugly (and huge) head, squinting against the sunlight, and looks around.

"Nothing down there, huh?"

But before Pete can punch me in the shoulder, or we can run like hell, the thing SPEAKS. I mean, it doesn't really talk, but you can hear it in your mind. It's loud as shit. Anyway, here's what it says:

BOK HAS RISEN.
WHO POSSESSES THE GLEAMING STONE?

"Wait. Did he say BOX?"
"No, BOK. Like a chicken. BOK BOK."
"Stupid name. But they were right about the legend. Hey, shouldn't we be leaving?"
I pull my backpack on a little tighter, getting ready to bolt, and right on cue the Controller falls out of the not-quite-fully-closed back pocket. Basically three pounds of solid Rhodium, the rarest metal on Earth. I watch it fall in slow motion.

C-L-U-N-K.

It's the loudest clunk of all time. Guinness-record-setting clunk. So loud that the entire crowd spins around and stares at me and Pete, and the Controller, with its pure, gleaming rhodium sitting there on the pavement.

And I suddenly make the connection: the Controller IS the Gleaming Stone.

BOK WILL ASK ONE MORE TIME.
WHO POSSESSES THE GLEAMING STONE?

And to answer the thing's question, every last one of these ungrateful New Yorkers lifts their finger and points at us. (Two seconds ago they're naming their kids after us, and now they're turning us over to BOK. Thanks, folks!) BOK's gaze follows their pointing fingers right to us and the Controller. And I don't know if it can smile, but if it can, it's definitely smiling right now. And licking its lips.

And in that moment, every fantasy I ever had about being one of the Fantastic Four, or saving a planet, or lifting a building to save some wounded blonde, goes out the window. All I can think is this:

Nah. Being a superhero SUCKS.

8
Wait, Let Me Back Up

From: Chip Collins
To: Julie Taylor
Date: June 4, 2015 5:43am
Wait, let me back up

Hi Julie,

Woah. Sorry. Got WAY ahead of myself, and realized I must sound like I'm dropping acid. Superheroes? Legend? Controller? BOK? Gleaming Stone? What the fuck?

So let me back up:

"Okay, Tesla. Where to?"

We figure out that the lost journal of Nikola Tesla is a two-way communication device to the man himself, which gives us a little hope and a clear, easy-to-remember goal:

Find Tesla. Go home.

I'm feeling good, like karma's back on my side. Life's going to get back to normal soon – Tesla just needs to give us directions to find him, then we break him out of some prison he's in (how hard can that be?), shoot back to dimension #234,698,594,394,683 (a.k.a. home-sweet-home), heat up that lasagna, get married, have a party, and live happily ever after. Boom. Done.

And then karma kicks me in the balls.

> "Dear Sir,
> Aha! A fellow traveler! Finally!
> Welcome to the INTERDIMENSIONAL
> TRANSFER APPARATUS. I am Nikola
> Tesla, its inventor. Before you embark
> on your own journeys, however, I
> would ask your assistance in extricating
> me from the prison mentioned in my
> previous journal entry. The coordinates
> are 59380918.593820e 482024.id.mt. Enter
> them into your INTERDIMENSIONAL
> NAVIGATION CONTROLLER and
> you should be here in less than a year.
> Perhaps even sooner if you utilize the
> shortcuts."

Wait - INTERDIMENSIONAL NAVI-*WHAT?!?*

Pete pretends to shoot himself in the head. Bobo does too (though it's pretty damn cute when Bobo does it).

> "Hey Tesla – you mind telling me what's
> an INTERDIMENSIONAL NAVIGATION
> CONTROLLER?"

> "It's the device that CONTROLS
> your INTERDIMENSIONAL
> NAVIGATION."

> "Duh. I got that much."

"Duh?"

"Never mind. Where's this controller?"

"I placed it on my desk, with instructions, right next to the copy of the journal you are reading. It is critical to the operation of the INTERDIMENSIONAL TRANSFER APPARATUS. You cannot find your way without it. If you don't have it already, simply return through the doorway you originally came through to retrieve it."

I turn to Pete. "Simply return through the doorway we originally came through? Doesn't he know we'd be RUNNING THROUGH THE FUCKING DOORWAY HOME and never coming back if we knew which doorway it was?"

Then something snaps with Pete, and he's got this wild look in his eyes (which might be cool, if it wasn't me he was looking at). "You know what? I've had enough. That book has screwed us for the last time. Give it to me."
"No, dude. Calm down."
"Now. Give it to me."
"Pete, you're upset. I understand. But we need the journal. It's our ticket home. Our only ticket."

But it's too late – Pete's rage switch is already on. He grabs the journal and we play tug-of-war with it. Bobo's jumping up trying to grab a piece too, I guess it looks like a fun game (he's still pretending to shoot himself in the head, btw). Then Pete snatches the book away from me and goes to rip it in half.

"NO!!" I grab it back, and stuff it down my pants. Wrong move. Pete's on me in a second like a rabid mountain lion (do mountain lions get rabies?), mauling me.

"Give me the goddamn book!"

We fall to the floor, me on my back and Pete right on my chest. I can't breathe. I'm trying to kick him off, and he's reaching around me for the book, and Bobo's psyched, because now the game just got even more fun, and he jumps on Pete's back, so now they're both on top of me.

"can't… breathe…"

Then suddenly, somewhere deep in the recesses of Pete's mind, I think he realizes he can't really trash the book, and we need Tesla, as much as he hates the idea, if we're ever going to find our way home. So he gets off me with a huff. "Whatever. It probably smells like your ass now anyway. Keep it."

But Bobo's not done with the game yet, and he keeps jumping up and down directly on my chest. Pete's enjoying this part – if he can't have the book, at least he can watch me slowly die at the hands of Bobo.

"get…"

Jump.

"the…"

Jump.

"fuck…"

Jump.

"off…"

Jump.

"me…"

Bobo's having the time of his life. But when Pete sees I'm about to pass out, he finally pulls him off. I curl up in a fetal position (it's getting to be a habit), wheezing. And Julie, the weirdest thought pops into my head while I'm trying to catch my breath: remember that time we went to Sleepy's Mattresses and started jumping up and down on that giant bed? It was like a trampoline. I remember watching you, your hair waving all over the place, getting in your mouth, I could barely see your eyes, but enough to see how you get those wrinkles in the corners when you're laughing hysterically. It was perfect, us jumping together in rhythm. (corny, I know, but it's my email and I'll write whatever the hell I want.) And then you pushed me, and I fell, and you crashed right onto my chest, laughing. And I couldn't breathe, but I didn't care. Because if that's how I was going to die, that's all right. That's exactly how I wanted to die. And then the guy came over and kicked us out of the store, but not before you whispered right in my ear "I like defying gravity with you." You're so weird.

"Hey. Earth to Chip. What the hell are you smiling at?"
"Uh. Nothing."

"Good. Then quit staring off into space and grinning like an idiot, and start turning this thing around with Tesla. Or next time, I don't care how much we need the book, I'm feeding it to Bobo."

Whoops. Right. Back to business.

> "Look, Tesla, dude, it's the year 2015. I found your journal in an old desk drawer. The FBI must have lost your Navigation Controller, too (I refuse to write it in all caps, btw). And you didn't think to mention it in the journal. To warn us that we'd need it. Nice move. So we're stuck. And you're stuck. So thanks for nothing. Now how about some actual help getting us all home?"

His response:

> "Hmmm."

Wow. He literally wrote "Hmmm." Instead of just saying it to himself. I would laugh, but the last time I laughed (see previous email) my appendix almost exploded. So we just kind of sit there waiting. Then suddenly the journal is scratching away like crazy. Uh-oh. Tesla's ticked.

> "Dear Sir,
> As my response is multi-part, I will employ a list:
> First: Do not call me 'dude.' I have never vacationed or labored at a ranch,

or railroad, or whatever that term might mean in your day. Call me Nikola.

Second: Though I am sorry to hear that the FBI has bungled the handling of the journal and the INTERDIMENSIONAL NAVIGATION CONTROLLER, I did not include instructions for it in the journal for one simple reason: because instructions were sitting right beside it! A second set of instructions? Highly inefficient!

Third: What does 'btw' mean? You will have to educate me on the vernacular of 2015. I guessed 'before the war,' and 'bring the washbasin,' but neither fit in context.

Fourth: This is most important. Do not consider yourself 'stuck.' Do not consider me 'stuck.' We are temporarily delayed. That is all. Nothing stops. Everything is temporary. We will simply have to build another INTERDIMENSIONAL NAVIGATION CONTROLLER together, for you to use."

I look up at Pete. "Well, at least he likes making lists."
"Yeah, you two should get along great. Just make sure the next list is *How to Build a Navigation Controller in Three Easy Steps Using Only a Plumber's Wrench.*"

So we write back and forth with Tesla, (btw, I explain what "btw" means – "by the way"– was it really that hard to figure out, Nikola?) and eventually he sends us a list of components, diagrams, and directions for assembling this Controller thing. Pete plops down next to me, and we both stare at the notes, scratching our heads.

"Uh, Pete. So what do you make of this?"
"Me?"
"You have the degree, dude."
"You have a degree too, you idiot. We graduated from the same college."
"Yeah, but my degree is in Philosophy. Useless."
"Not totally useless. It helped you get into that girl Carla's pants."
"True. True. But we don't need to get into Tesla's pants. We need a Controller thing. You the man."
"Dude - my degree is in finance. So unless the Controller is made out of Convertible Preferred Stocks, we might as well have Bobo here build it." We both turn to Bobo.

Blink. Blink.

"Yup. We're fucked."

From: Chip Collins
To: Julie Taylor
Date: June 4, 2015 5:43am
Re: Wait, let me back up

Hi Julie,

You're probably thinking we're fucked too (and generally, I'd agree with you). Building one of these Controller things? Good luck. But then it hits me. "Wait! Brainstorm!"
"Uh-oh."
"No, dude. Really. Listen, it's a quick cab ride to Columbia University from the hotel. First, we find a friendly dimension. Then we shoot up there and grab the chairman of the electrical engineering department. He'll be able to make sense of this. Then we get him to build this thing for us. Easy peasy."
"Yeah. Sounds like it'll happen just like that."
"Right. Right?"
"Not a fucking chance. No one will believe us, and even if they do, what makes you think they'd actually help us? *Hi, we're two guys from another dimension, and we need you to stop what you're doing and put yourself in harm's way. We have three hundred dollars, which probably doesn't even mean anything in your dimension. Oh, and a plumber's wrench.*"
"Okay, smart guy. Your turn. Blow me away."
"A-HEM. Easy. We find a dimension where the Controller is still sitting there on the desk. We take it. Done."
Hmm. It does sound easy. I'm all about easy. "Cool. My plan sucked anyway."

Fast forward a full day (or week, or month, like I said, time doesn't pass in here so it could've been a year), and me and Pete haven't found shit. Well, we've found lots of dangerous shit, and all kinds of weird shit, but not the shit we're looking for. Shit, shit, shit.

"Dude? I hate to admit this, but remember your plan that sucked?"
"Yeah?"
"I'm starting to think it didn't suck so much."
I smile. "Well, I don't mean to brag, but…"
"Don't get ahead of yourself. It still sucks. Just not as much. Maybe we should give it a shot."
So we ditch the current sucky plan, and go with my slightly-less-sucky plan (*Columbia University > get smart person > build controller > save Tesla >* live happily ever after). At least we're scratching notes into the doors, so it's easy to find one that leads to the hotel room.

"Bingo. Let's go. Bobo, you stay here."

Bobo's way ahead of me I guess, because he's not even paying attention – he's just sitting there nibbling on a piece of lint from his fur. So me and Pete step through (ever-so-gently, we're learning quick that we could be stepping into our own graves) into Room 3327.

Pete heads in first, takes one step, and launches straight up to the ceiling, hitting his head. Bonk.

WTF?

As he comes down, he laces into a string of profanities so long and explicit I'm too embarrassed to write it down here (yeah, I know, my virgin ears, right?). But it makes me laugh, which I know is the absolute worst thing I could do when Pete's pissed off.

"You think it's funny? Get in here, Mister Laugh-a-Minute. Let's see how you do."

And sure enough, even though I KNOW it's coming, I step in and do the SAME EXACT thing. Bonk. "Ouch! Motherfucker!" (Julie, I swear that's like a children's school prayer compared to what Pete said before.)

Now Pete's laughing, and pointing up. My head actually left a dent in the ceiling. And after we both finish rubbing our heads, we notice we can barely keep our feet on the ground. We're light as a feather. Crazy, right?

I blurt out "lighter gravity."

And Pete does a little double-take. "Okay, I'm a little scared that I'm saying this, but I think you're right. You must have knocked something into place in your brain there."

I punch him in the arm, and he goes shooting across the room into the wall.

"Woah! Cool!"

"Hey, you know what lighter gravity means, right? *The Matrix!*"

So we immediately start doing *Matrix* moves on each other, flips and shit, laughing and hitting the walls and the ceiling, smacking each other with the pillows and making them all explode, and then some poor woman in the next hotel room is like "Hey! What's going on in there?! Do I have to call the cops?"

We freeze. The word "cops" causes a Pavlov reaction: we're so scared of running into Evil Cop again, we immediately stop everything. Pete drops his plumber's wrench with a thud.

"SHHHH!"

"You Shhh! That was like the loudest 'Shhh' I've ever heard."

"You want to hear a loud 'Shhh'? Loud like your stupid fucking wrench?"

"No. Just shut the fuck up!"

"SHHHHHH!"

Hours (okay, a few seconds) later, we finally calm down and get ready to leave. But it's nighttime, and nobody's rented the room, so we decide to crash and start out tomorrow.

Goodnight, Julie. xoxoxo

From: Chip Collins
To: Julie Taylor
Date: June 4, 2015 5:43am
Re: Wait, let me back up

Hi Julie,

Man, I slept great. Like in the hallway, time doesn't pass, so you don't need sleep, but psychologically, you do need it, so you're always in this state of wanting a nap even though you're not tired. Yawning for no reason. Like right now. Yawn. (Did you catch my yawn?)

Anyway, next morning (who knows, it could've been days – we slept like grizzly bears), we start down to the lobby. And Julie, you would post this to Videos-Of-Morons.com if you could see how we're walking. We're putting almost no pressure on the ground, and we're practically floating. It's exactly like walking on the moon (I know from all my prior moonwalking experience). In order not to go bounding into the air, every step has to be a gentle arch, like a cartoon character trying to walk through a minefield. We also find out it works better if we sort of hold each other down while the other one takes a step, so my left hand is on his right shoulder, and his right hand is on my left shoulder. Quite the picture. Pete's not happy.

"Just quit giggling. You're making it worse."

So I try to stifle my giggles (which is really impossible now that he's saying not to do it), and we make it out onto the street. I hail a cab, and Pete grabs the door handle to open it for me. What a nice guy.

Then he rips the door off the hinge.

"Oops."

The cabbie gets out and runs around to give Pete a piece of his mind, but he stops cold. Now you know Pete's in good shape – especially compared to me – but compared to this cab guy? He's Thor. (Except with a big wrench instead of a hammer.)

Chip's Quick List of Things to Know About This Dimension:

- It's got lighter gravity. Because our muscles are built for much heavier gravity, we can fly. Well, not fly, but bound around like the Hulk. Like literally jump a mile. (Pete tried it. It was awesome.)

- Everyone's scrawny. Like same height as us, but thirty or forty pounds tops. We figure because of the gravity, people don't need as much muscle. Hardly any, really. So to them we look like demigods. (Okay, Pete looks like a demigod, and I look like whatever is a couple of steps down from a demigod.)

- Objects are brittle and weak. We figure
  (*Hey, look at us, Julie – we're figuring stuff out!)*
  because people are weak, they need their stuff
  to be proportionately lightweight – car doors,
  toasters, manhole covers, etc.)

So anyway, the cabbie has totally changed his tune, and
he's like "Uh, uh, excuse me, sorry, sir. Y-Y-You can just put
that in the trunk. A-And the fare's on me. Where to?"

But before Pete can even answer, we notice up the block
something's causing a commotion (God, I love that word,
commotion. It's like not quite an emergency, it's almost
goofy, like "those circus clowns over there are causing
a commotion juggling those chainsaws.") Anyway, the
commotion actually does turn out to be an emergency:
a bunch of people are looking up and shouting for
help. About fifteen stories up this building, a couple of
bricklayers are hanging on for dear life to some scaffolding,
and it looks like the whole thing's gonna come crashing
down any second.

Without a word, Pete immediately leaps up the building
(did I mention it's fifteen stories?) and plucks the workers
off the scaffolding just as it gives way. But the whole thing,
along with a huge pile of bricks stacked on the planks,
starts falling toward the ground.

Oh shit.

People on sidewalk.
Mom with double stroller.

Two business guys.

No time to think.

I hurl myself towards them.

In midair (it's true: stuff like this feels like it happens in super slow motion), I pull out the Shogun, press button four – force field – and fling it at the stroller. Then I barrel into the two guys, grabbing them and turning, so my back crashes through a deli window, and we all land inside just before the scaffolding and shit smashes into the sidewalk. Dust everywhere. Can't see. I rush outside. The mom…

It worked.

Julie, holy cow, something I did actually worked!

The mom and her twins are inside the bubbled safety of the force field from the Shogun. *Whew.* The two guys stumble out of the deli, brushing off their suits, without a scratch. *Whew again.* And Pete jumps down from the side of the building, a worker under either arm. He sets them down, looks at me and smiles.

"Dude. Was that YOU?"

"I guess. Who knew?"

"Kick ass. You're my hero."

The crowd around us is in total silence. They have no idea what the hell just happened. Then one guy starts clapping. And another. Pretty soon everyone's clapping, hooting, coming over and hugging us. Cops are shooting their guns in the air (not really, but that would be awesome, wouldn't it?). It's great, I'll admit it. We're soaking it in. We're in the zone. I go over to Pete to give him a hug. He backs up.

"Don't ruin it, dude."

Clink. Clink. Clink.

Whoops. It's the lady in the bubble, tapping on it. She's obviously grateful, tears and everything, but she's also like "Um, are you ever going to get us out of here?"

Me and Pete look at each other, then back at the mom. Shrug. Sorry, lady. It'll be at least a half hour, based on our past Bobo tests. It's a buzz kill, I know, but you're alive, right?

But she's not waiting. She's trapped in a force field bubble with twins crying their heads off, and I'm sure it's getting hot in there. And I have no idea about the oxygen situation. So she leans down and presses a random button on the Shogun.

"NO!!! I mean, COULDN'T YOU ASK FIRST?! You could kill yourself! Or your kids! I mean, what the hel..."

And the field trap instantly disappears.

"...huh. So that's what button five does."

I mean, of course. It took me and Pete HOURS to test all this shit on Bobo, waiting for the effects of the Shogun to wear off every time, instead of just trying button five. Duh. Well, now we know for next time. Thanks, random mom.

Anyway, now that she's free, she's back to realizing we saved her and her kids, and she leaps into my arms (don't worry Julie, I'm not hot for scrawny moms of twins from other dimensions, or anybody but you for that matter, schnookums), and the crowd goes wild. WILD. (Btw, this hero stuff should definitely get me a lower score on your douche-meter, right?)

So we do our best rock-star waves to the adoring throngs and make our exit, while everybody's still kind of in shock, and the *Good Morning New York* cameras are just getting there (I'm like "Dude, cameras!" and Pete's like "No. FOCUS, dude."), and we head uptown in our doorless cab. I'm sitting there smiling, and Pete knows exactly what I'm thinking.

"No. We aren't superheroes."
I'm not listening. "What's going to be your superhero name?"
"We're not superheroes."
"Come on dude. Don't kill the moment. Whatever. Humor me. IF you were a superhero, what would your name be?"
"I don't know. Fly Guy. No. The Brute."
"Cool. For me I'm thinking Awesome Man."
"Modest. I like it. Subtle. As always."

So Awesome Man and The Brute get out at Columbia University (after The Brute reattaches the cabbie's door with his bare hands – awww, The Brute's really just a softy), and we stroll (if you can call the herky-jerky thing we have to do to stay on the ground 'strolling') right past staring security guards and professors, to the Office of the Department of Electrical Engineering. Nobody even asks us a question. We must be giving off the superhero glow. It's awesome. Just like Awesome Man, right?

Ding!

I tap the little bell at the reception desk and flatten it into a pancake. Whoops. Awesome Man needs to control his awesomeness a little better.

The receptionist girl (nice looking, nerdy-but-cool glasses, scrawny as hell like everyone else we've met) is sitting right there watching this, so I don't even know why I dinged the bell, but she takes it down like a wounded bird, puts it in a drawer for a little mini-funeral, and glares at me.

"Can I help you?"
"Yes. We'd like to speak with the department chair."
"Sorry. Mrs. Herbert's not in." (She says this with some definite relish, btw, like *"Ha. That's for the bell, asshole."*)
"We can wait. When will she be back?"
"Two weeks. She's on vacation." (Again with the relish!)
Pete takes over, and wouldn't you know it, his Thor vibe is still working its magic. The second she notices him, the smirk disappears and she's all dimples and eyelashes.
"Listen, my friend ~~Awesome Man~~ Chip and I are in a bit of a jam, and we really need Mrs. Herbert's help getting home."

I'm thinking this girl must be having a seizure, her eyelashes are fluttering so much. "Well, she's overseas, so there's really no way to track her down. But maybe I can help you. I'm her T&A."
I snort laugh. I can't help it. I'm so juvenile. (You're allowed to smack me for that one when we get back.) Anyway, she glares at me again, this time with extra relish.

"Her TEACHER & ASSISTANT, sir. And Doctoral Student. With a 4.2 grade point. With a Tesla Award on my shelf, if you don't mind."

Our jaws drop. "Wait. Did you say Tesla Award?"

"Yes. Named in honor of Nikola Tesla, for outstanding contribution to the field of electricity and electronics. First person under thirty-five ever to receive it. Don't act so surprised, gentleman. Girls are allowed to be smart."

"No, no. It's not that you're a girl. It's that we KNOW Tesla."

She scowls. "I said I was SMART, gentlemen, not GULLIBLE. Tesla died in 1943. He'd be ah… 158 years, 10 months, and 25 days old…" she looks at her watch, "yes, that's it… if he were alive. Don't take me for a fool. Now if you've had your fun, good day."

She gets up, pissed, and starts herding us towards the door. But there's no way I'm letting her get away – she's the one. She just calculated Tesla's age to the day. In her head. I can't even remember if it's Daylight Savings Time.
"Wait."
"Wait *what*."
"Take a look at this first, before you kick us out." I pull out the journal and plop it on the counter.

She considers it for a second. "Where did you get this?"
Me and Pete look at each other. It's going to be a long afternoon.

From: Chip Collins
To: Julie Taylor
Date: June 4, 2015 5:43am
Re: Wait, let me back up

Hi Julie,

A MILLION HOURS LATER...

Shit, by the end of our story, even Pete and I can hardly believe everything that's happened so far. So I'm not surprised she's skeptical.

"I'm sorry, I'm still not convinced. How do I know with certainty you're telling the truth? That this isn't some kind of elaborate scheme to build a weapon or something? What hard evidence is there that you've been to other dimensions?"

Hard evidence. Hmmm. Wait – the Shogun. Of course! I pull it out and smack it on the desk. "Exhibit A." (Awesome - I've always wanted to say that. Chip the District Attorney.)

She looks it over. "Hmm. Very interesting. What's this button do?"

And before I can scream "WHY DOESN'T ANYONE ASK BEFORE TOUCHING THE GODDAMN BUTTONS?!," before I can lunge at her to rip it away, before Pete can block her curious index finger, she presses the first button. But I'm already in mid-lunge, so I can't stop, so my hand touches the tip.

THWUNK.

9
Ouch.
My Head Hurts.

From: Chip Collins
To: Julie Taylor
Date: June 4, 2015 5:43am
Ouch. My head hurts.

Hi Julie,

Where the hell am I? And God. What a headache.

Like forget any headaches I had before this. Like forget the headache I got when we went to that go-kart place and I thought I was Mario Andretti but I wound up tipping the stupid car and banging my head on the retaining wall. But you were great, I mean you were laughing at me, but you pulled me from the wreck (okay, I'm exaggerating, but it sounds better than 'lifted my sorry ass out of the mini go-kart'), and you got ice from the machine for me, and kissed me on my forehead, and instead of go-karts we tried to win that big stuffed football from the claw machine for two hours. You know I still have that thing? I mean, I better, it cost fifty bucks in quarters.

Actually, I have lots of stuff from that summer. I have the ticket stub from the Knicks playoff game (remember those awesome seats? We were only like four rows from Woody Allen, and we tried to get his attention the whole time instead of watching the game). And those t-shirts we made, with the big "4EVA" on them and the cut-off sleeves. Do you still have yours? Do you still have anything? Or did you throw it all in a trash can and set it on fire?

You know, I wouldn't blame you.

How could I? I never was as good to you as you deserved (yes, I know, NOW I realize it, when you're some infinite number of dimensions away from me). You were always there for me, for two years, and I just kind of let that be the way it worked. So I wouldn't blame you for letting this time be the last straw. Letting it all burn.

But I wish I could take it back. I wish the goddamn Tesla hallway wasn't a dimension machine, but a time machine, so I could go back and instead of saying "I need a little space" or whatever stupid shit I said, I could say "FORGET space, babe - let's stay together forever!" I mean, what did I think? Did I think I was going to meet someone better for me? Did I think some other superficial quality, or one less pet peeve, or being alone, could make me happier? What am I, an idiot? (Rhetorical, no need to answer that.)

But you know what? Maybe this whole thing with Tesla is a test. A test with just one question: "Question 1. Hey, Chip, what the fuck do you REALLY want? You've got infinite possibilities, so what's it gonna be? Make a choice and stick with it, dude." So maybe I'm not a lost cause. Maybe I'll pass the test. Maybe you'll stick around when I get back and give me another chance. We'll see.

Wait, where the hell am I again?

Right. The *Shogun*. Frozen (button one) and passed-out for God-knows-how-long. Laying on the floor (yes, in the fetal position again), with grenades exploding against my temples. Ouch.

I look up. "Need... Ice..."

"Ahh. You're back. Good. We were just going over the components we'll need."

"Ice... Please..."

"Yeah, ice, sure, whatever. Hey, is your brain okay? We need you to focus, dude. Get up."

"Guess I'm fetching my own damn ice, huh?" I mutter to myself, and as I get up, of course I forget that we're in lighter gravity, so of course I launch up to the ceiling and hit my fucking head again. Even Receptionist/Tesla Award-Winner Girl laughs. Nice. I rub my new bump (I'm starting a collection), and now it's my turn to glare.

"Funny, huh, Miss..."

"Thatcher. Margaret Thatcher."

"Wait. Margaret Thatcher? Cool! Like the Prime Minister." She gives me a blank look.

"Of England."

"What's England?"

"The country. In Europe."

"What's Europe?"

"It's– forget it."

Chip's Quick List of Things to Know About This Dimension – Additional Entry:

• There's no Europe. Go figure.

"In any case, you can call me Meg." (Did she just wink at Pete? Or is that just more uncontrollable eyelash waving?) "Okay, Meg. Listen, first – that age guessing thing you did was cool. Can you just randomly do that? Like say my friend Pete here was born on June 4, 1985."

"I'd say Happy Birthday. He was born exactly 30 years ago today. Too easy."

Wait. That can't be right.

Today's June 4. Yes. And... Pete's birthday... is June 4.

FUCK.

I forgot. Again.

And I didn't just forget. I talked Pete into stepping into the Interdimensional Transfer Apparatus, and saying goodbye forever to his normal, content life ON HIS THIRTIETH BIRTHDAY.

I whip my head around to Pete (almost passing out from the pain of my brain hitting the inside of my skull). And he can see the gears turning furiously in my head, the calculations: how many Pete birthdays have I forgotten? Or worse, how many Pete birthdays have I forgotten AND made him buy beers? All I can manage to say is "Jeez. I can't believe it's been a year since I forgot your last birthday."

He just pats me on the shoulder and smiles. "Thirty. Whatever. I didn't remember either, dude. You can get me a cake when we get back."

Man, is Pete great or what? I ruined his life, and he lets me off the hook. "Definitely. Big cake. Ice cream with crunchies. Happy birthday, The Brute."

Now it's Meg's turn to ruin the moment. "Sorry to interrupt your very strange and awkward birthday celebration, but can we get back to the list? There are some pretty interesting things on here."

Fifty-three "Pretty Interesting Things" Needed to Build the Interdimensional Navigation Controller:

1. 1,250 grams Rhodium (I know, what the hell is that)

2. Primary Capacitor 20kV (same here, wtf?)

3. Sliding Magnetic Shield (same here, wtf?)

4. Stator (same here, wtf?)

5. Flux Capacitor (kidding! Just wanted to see if you were paying attention)

6-53. Blah, blah, blah, boring technical stuff. Trust me, Meg saying "pretty interesting things" was a major overstatement.

Okay, anyway, we read through the list (or actually Meg reads through the list and we almost nod off from boredom), she's poring through all the diagrams and shit, and then, she's like "Gentlemen. I have good news and bad news."

I wipe the drool from the corner of my mouth. (Did I say *almost* nod off?) "Uh, whatever. Just give us the worst news first. We're getting used to it."

"The bad news is the rhodium. Rhodium is a rare metal, a hundred times rarer than gold, and priced appropriately. That's almost three pounds of rhodium for an anti-corrosive and super-conductive shell around the core of the unit.

My guess at market price is a thousand dollars a gram, so that would be a million dollars, give or take."

"Gee, only a million dollars? What's the bad news?"

"…And the supply isn't concentrated anywhere, so good luck finding that much rhodium for sale in one place."

"Fuck. Okay, on to the good news. Please tell me your dad owns a rhodium dealership."

"No, the good news was going to be that the actual construction of the Controller is not only possible, but with current electronics that Tesla didn't have available in 1943, very straightforward. The brain of the unit could be your average smartphone."

"Great. So one iPhone and a million dollars worth of rhodium gets us a Controller."

"Well… of course there'd be my fee, too. Half up front. And the patent rights."

I practically jump out of my chair to strangle her, but Pete holds me back. He's smiling. And it hits me:

Pete's digging her!

Of course! She's smart as hell, problem-solver type, good-looking (as the scrawny folk here go), and now add to that she's all business-negotiation-veins-of-ice, and Pete's over the moon. Damn.

"Chip, c'mon. Let's hear her out."

Meg clears her throat. "Thank you, Pete." (*Hey, quit with the eyelashes, Meg!*) "As I was saying, all of this is dangerous. Obtaining the rhodium, building the device, testing it. I need a fee to cover not only my time, and my time away from the office, but also the danger involved. Also, I've got student loans to pay off, and a career to think about.

And what did you think – I would just do this out of the goodness of my heart?"

"Uh… yes?"

"Sorry."

Pete's still enthralled, but I've heard enough. "Okay, whatever. Get to the bottom line."

"Patent rights for the device forever. And a hundred thousand dollars."

Pete spits out his water. I take my wallet out. "Hey, no problem! I've got my American Express Rhodium card right here."

Pete kicks me under the table. "Sorry, Meg. You'll have to excuse Chip here, it's just his way of coping with shitty situations. But he's got a point – even if we could come up with your fee, isn't the rhodium a no-go?"

"It would seem. Legally, anyway. But there is *something*."

We both lean forward. Hmm. Sounds juicy.

"Well. There is a meteorite in the gem collection at the Smithsonian in Washington D.C. I saw it several years ago. Called the *Gleaming Stone*."

"The Gleaming Stone?"

"Yes. Named after an ancient legend about a demon who becomes all powerful when the stone is near. *The Demon and the King*. It's a children's story. You'd like it, Chip."

I give Meg the finger. She just looks at in blankly. I guess they don't have the finger in their dimension either. No Europe. No finger. Check.

"In any case, the meteorite's almost a hundred percent rhodium, and it's nearly five pounds. Since no one can lift it, it's in an open display where visitors can touch it."

"Wait. No one can lift five pounds?"

"Chip. Lighter gravity, dude."

"Ahhhh! That means me and Pete could just waltz in and – wait. You want us to steal a meteorite from the government?"

"I don't want you to do anything. You told me you want to go home."

Again, that word *home*. *HOME*. It weakens our righteousness. "Well, I mean it's just a rock, right? It's not doing anyone any good just sitting there. It behooves us to put it to good use. For the greater good. Yeah."

Pete's nodding, he's already way ahead of me. "We'll be extremely careful. Now about your fee. There has to be something else we can work out. We just don't have that kind of money."

I get another brainstorm (weird, I know, multiple brainstorms in one day). "No, dude. We don't have that kind of money YET. I have an idea."

"Great. Another idea."

"Yes. I have great ideas. All the time."

"Yeah. Like 'hey Pete, let's check out this dimension thing on your birthday'."

"Man - already? It's not even three minutes, and you're pulling out the birthday guilt?"

He grins. "Get used to it."

I decide to ignore him, and start making a phone call (my phone works here – another go-figure). Pete tries to grab for it. "I know what you're thinking. Hang up. Alternate Chip and Pete from this dimension aren't going to have a hundred thousand dollars."

"Of course not. I wasn't calling them." The phone rings and picks up.

"Hello? Yes, is this *Good Morning New York*? I have some information on the two men who saved a bunch of people in midtown earlier... Yes, the flying ones... Sure, I'll hold for the producer... Hi, yes, the flying men who saved all those people this morning? That's us... What? Sure, we'd love to come on the show..."

Pete's angry, hitting my arm, swiping at the phone, saying something about what a selfish asshole I am, this is the worst possible time to go stroking my own ego and chasing some cheap celebrity, blah, blah, blah. He's not getting it.

"...Tomorrow? Sure... Of course, there's our *fee*..."

And Pete stops grabbing for the phone, and smiles.

10
I Was On
Good Morning New York!

From: Chip Collins
To: Julie Taylor
Date: June 4, 2015 5:43am
I was on *Good Morning New York*!

Hi Julie,

So while Meg starts building what she can of the Interdimensional Navigation Controller (man, we need a cooler name for that), me and Pete embark on my favorite part of this whole thing so far:

> Awesome Man and The Brute's
> Superhero Celebrity Tour.

I'm not ashamed to admit it – I love the attention. TV show hosts, reporters, shit – EVERYONE is dying to talk to us, to touch the magic. And until we hit our hundred thousand dollar fundraising goal, there's going to be plenty of magic to go around. We're doing TV, radio, print, live public demonstrations of our powers – I know, total whores. Whatever. Bring it on.

There's one thing that's kind of pissing me off, though. Pete keeps taking off here and there to visit his crush Meg. Ugh. Probably talking about money and working out and shit. It reminds me of that girl he took camping with us. Rebecca or something. He was totally into her, taking off with her into the woods every chance he had, but you and me got shitfaced and carved that bow and arrow out of a couple

of sticks and sort of accidentally shot her in the calf.
We never saw her after that. No wonder he doesn't want
me around when he visits Meg. Doesn't want her shot in
the leg. Good. I've got more important thing to take care of.
I don't really like her. Can you tell?

Anyway, the highlight moment of the week? Our first
interview on *Good Morning New York* with Sandy Maytime:

"Gentlemen, so where are you from? Another planet?
Someplace on Earth that hasn't been discovered? Were you
exposed to cosmic radiation, or an experimental drug?"

Pete fields the question first. "Well, I wish it was something
exciting like that. But really we're just a couple of guys who
are a little different, trying to get home."

Uh, Pete? That was booooorrrriiiinnnngggg.

Sandy flatlines. Only two people in the entire studio
audience clap. This is embarrassing. So I jump in.
"Well, uh, Sandy, that's... our cover story. See, we're not
supposed to tell the truth. It's too huge. It could have
universe-wide ramifications."
Sandy's heart starts beating again, and she practically falls
off her stool. Now THIS is exciting. "Oooh. Perhaps just a
hint? Please?"
"Well, Sandy, I could get in trouble for this..." Sandy smells
a scoop "...but okay. We are, in fact, from another planet,
on a mission of peace and protection."
Pete rolls his eyes, but there's nothing else he can do – we're
in front of a bunch of cameras, the audience is finally tuning
in, and I'm on a roll.

"Our planet, uh, Xircon, is many millions of light years away. We were chosen from among thousands of top Alliance Officers to visit Earth. You see, your world is very special."

The audience is gripping their armrests. Sandy's panting.

"Our world? Us? Special? Why?"

"I really shouldn't."

If Sandy could personally write me a check for a hundred thousand dollars right now, she would. Not only am I giving her the first interview with two Alliance Officers visiting Earth, but I'm about to tell her, and her audience, and the world watching her show, and the advertisers paying for 30-second spots, why Earth is so darn special.

"Please, continue!"

"Well, all right. We have seen many worlds. But yours has more potential than any, more capacity for greatness. In fact, a great leader will rise from your people. A great leader! But there is one thing."

Pete's looking at me like I've lost my mind, doing his not-so-subtle hand-slicing-across-the-throat move. And really, I have no idea where this story is headed. I'm like a demented, rambling storyteller from another planet (didn't you actually call me that once?), with no ending in sight. I just keep talking and talking and talking, and now I've talked myself into a corner. I'm stuck.

"And?" Sandy pleads.

"There is one thing."

"You said that already. Please."

"And that one thing is…"

Pete jumps in.

"Rhodium."

Oh my God. Pete's a fucking genius.

Forget stealing the meteorite – if Pete pulls this off, they'll *give* it to us!

"Excuse me? Rhodium?"

"Yes, rhodium. A very rare metal here on your planet. Our readings show a concentration of over five pounds in Washington D.C., possibly a meteorite. There is a terrible creature searching the cosmos for such large concentrations, and we've been sent to retrieve it. To protect you from this creature's wrath."

Sandy's swooning. "Ooohhh! Like the children's legend about the demon and the king."

"Uh. Yes."

I'm like come on, Pete, "Uh, yes?" Not exactly the most rousing ending, dude. The producer's counting down to a commercial, the audience is frothing at the mouth, and we need a little Awesome Man polish. So I hop off my stool and raise both fists into the air.

"Yes, Sandy. Like the children's legend. Good people of Earth, your safety is our mission. A legend is just a legend. But greatness is real. AND GREATNESS IS YOUR DESTINY!"

MAYHEM.

Julie, people are passing out in the aisles, cheering for us, and for themselves, hugging total strangers, crossing themselves, you name it. Sandy's wiping back tears. And the producer is standing next to the camera with a shit-eating grin and both thumbs up; he's thinking: *next stop, daytime Emmys!*

On our way back to the green room, people are crowding us for autographs, taking cell phone videos, and Pete turns to me and smiles. "You're welcome."

"Thanks, The Brute. Now let's go get us some rhodium."

11
About That
Meteorite…

From: Chip Collins
To: Julie Taylor
Date: June 4, 2015 5:43am
About that meteorite…

Hi Julie,

So the show went great. And the celebrity superhero tour was a blast. A hundred grand. Safe deposit box. Check. But our meeting with the government brass about taking their meteorite?

Not our best moment.

So me and Pete are sitting in your totally typical what-you-would-imagine government conference room – drab, maps on the wall, little American flags on the conference table. Four guys walk in. Two suits and two military. Big guns.

Julie, last week I was a security guard, with a badge on my shoulder a third-grader wouldn't take seriously. This week I'm meeting with the FBI and some big muckety-muck general with lots of stars and stripes and shit. So I'm kind of star struck, and I instinctively stand up and salute.

"You don't have to salute, son. You're a civilian. Oh, wait. You're an 'Alliance Officer' from another galaxy. So yes, go ahead, knock yourself out."

Uh-oh. I'm not getting the *sure-take-our-meteorite-we'll-gift-wrap-it-for-you* vibe that I was expecting.

The general leans right in, and does all the talking. No bullshit with this guy.

"First off, let's have that little shiny remote control thing of y'alls. And the wrench. No weapons allowed in the building, thank you very much."

Okay, bad vibe number two. They're taking our shit. But we need the damn rhodium even more, so we pony up our bad-ass superhero weapons. (Well, my Shogun was *bad-ass*. Pete's wrench was more *goofy-but-sure-as-hell-gets-the-job-done*.)

"Thank you gentlemen." Now he leans in even closer.

"So let me get this straight: you expect us to believe that you two clowns are from another planet, and y'all need to take our rhodium meteorite to protect us from an imaginary monster in a kid's story, so that we humans can achieve our destiny and send forth a great leader into the universe."

"Well, it does sound kind of far-fetched the way you're saying it."

"You're damned right it does. How would you say it?"

"Well, I would say… I would start with… uh, Pete?"

I turn around, and Julie – Pete is actually rolling his chair away from me! Like he's trying to slowly escape out the door without anyone noticing. Thanks, dude.

"I don't think your friend Pete here is an Alliance Officer either, are you Pete?"

Pete stops rolling and just looks down at the cheese danishes they put out for us. (They were actually pretty good, better than you'd expect.) I guess I'm on my own.

"But… look at us! Look at what we can do! We're clearly not from here!"

"See, there's where we can agree. Y'all are most definitely not from around here. You can fly, for Christ's sake. But another planet? Come on, son. I think we both know where you're from. And I think I know what you need the rhodium for."

"I have no clue what you're talking about."

The general presses a button in front of him, and another grunt walks in, pushing in a table with wheels. (He's huffing and puffing, the poor guy, even though the table weighs max ten pounds.) The general nods, so the grunt stops, and lifts the cover of the box on the table.

It's an Interdimensional Navigation Controller.

Just like the diagrams. Sitting right there in the middle of the table.

"Now do you have a clue, son?"

From: Chip Collins
To: Julie Taylor
Date: June 4, 2015 5:43am
Re: About that meteorite…

Hi Julie,

So we're totally snagged. It was a terrible lie, we're awful at it, so of course we've been found out. For a few minutes, though, I was holding it together, feeling like all this danger and excitement has made me a more courageous guy. Heck, I can take this guy's shit, this General Dickhead (he never introduced himself, but I'm sure that's his name, or it's close). What's so scary about him?

But the second he trots out the controller, I revert right back to my natural instincts.

I burst into tears.

"G-General, sir. (sobbing) We- We're just a couple of guys trying to get back to our dimension. I'm really sorry about lying to get the rhodium… (more sobbing) We just needed it to build… that."
Now I'm really blubbering, so General Dickhead hands me a hankie from his pocket. I blow my nose in it and hand it back. "Thank you, sir."
He waves it off – guess he's not keen on a pocketful of Chip snot – "No problem. Heck, who even needs a rhodium meteorite now? You can have this here pre-built controller! Free. It's on us."

Me and Pete look at each other. Is he serious?

"Are you serious?"

"Sure, son. Take us back to Room 3327 with y'all, get us into that Interdimensional Transfer Apparatus, and you're free to go. Go home."

"Wait. So you know about all this? Everything about Tesla?"

"Sure. Of course. We've got the journal. And this here controller. Everything. They don't know about it in your dimension?"

"No. The FBI lost the journal and the controller. They're total morons."

The FBI agent sitting next to me chokes on his danish and glares. Sorry, truth hurts sometimes, dude.

General Dickhead smiles. "Well, we didn't lose either one of them. Heck, we've even got eyes on that hotel 24/7. Got to see your little pillow fight the other night, too. Cute. Oh, and you both snore, by the way."

"It wasn't a pillow fight. We were testing out the gravit- hey, you've been watching us this whole time?"

"Shit sure, yes. I didn't even have the boys here pick you up until today, I was having so much fun keepin' an eye on y'all this week. You're a hoot."

"Not cool."

"Ha! You think I care about 'not cool?'" He leans in even closer (how close can this guy lean?). "Now listen up, and listen up good: with the intel and the resources you're going to lead us to, like more of those shiny little weapon thingys, you get your trip home. We win. You win."

"Intel? Resources? Weapons? What are you talking about?"

"Shit son, wake up. Don't you know what's going on? Haven't you turned on a TV since you've been here?"

Pete and I shake our heads. We haven't had time to _watch_ any TV – because we've been _on TV_, bitches!

"…well if you had turned on a TV, or read a newspaper, or paid any attention at all, you'd know we're at WAR, son! A war for FREEDOM! If we don't subjugate the rest of the world, how can everyone have the freedom they deserve? A freedom they don't even know they want? AMERICAN FREEDOM?" He catches himself going into a frenzy, and tones it down a notch. "But TECHNOLOGY wins wars. So you're going to get us what we need to win."

I'm not liking the sound of the word "subjugate" (remind me to look up what it means later), and it's sounding like he's giving me orders (fuck that), so my courage ticks up a little. "So why don't you just go yourself? Why do you need us?"

"Can't. We haven't figured out the combination to that damned lock!"

Come on. It's impossible.

The whole U.S. military/industrial/intelligence complex can't figure out 0-0-0-0? "It's not rocket science, General. It's actually pretty fucking obvious."

"Don't try my patience, son. 0-0-0-0? 1-2-3-4? What do you think, we're idiots? It was the first thing they tried, back in '43. Tried every goddamn integer combination. Every decimal combination to eight places. Nothing."

> **Meg's Official Theory on the**
> **ITA Lock Combination:**
> Why are we the only people in the ITA other than
> Tesla, if other people have tried 0-0-0-0? Meg's
> theory: our home dimension is the ONLY ONE
> with a combination of 0-0-0-0. So wherever we go,
> our combination somehow travels with us, like
> a personal dimension ID or something. And the
> other dimensions' combinations must be numbers
> between the digits, like 1.235952346920234098, so
> they're virtually impossible to guess, and even
> harder to dial in on those little manual luggage-lock
> dials. So if you're from this light gravity dimension,
> your combination might be 4.948300298765493812
> - 8.857466200193823219 - 1.868473629911204934
> - 0.958433772898431340. In other words, fucking
> impossible to crack, or to get just right on the dials.
> But me and Pete? 0-0-0-0 clicks right in. Boom.
> Meg's so smart. It pisses me off.

"But if you open the door for us, we can follow you right
in." He holds up the Shogun and admires it. "And get our
hands on some primo-grade weaponry. Or an army of folks
like you with superpowers. Bingo!"
"No. I don't think Tesla wanted the ITA to be used for
war stuff. Actually I'm sure of it. Tesla wanted to light the
world, not darken it."
General Dickhead pounds his fist on the table. "Fuck Tesla!"

Wait. Did this asshole just say "Fuck Tesla?"

I stand up, fists clenched. I mean, Tesla's not my favorite
flavor right now either, but at least he's trying to help us.

General Dickhead is just a douchebag, trying to use us to get his war rocks off. To do whatever *subjugate* is to the rest of the world. Screw that.

Anyway, Pete's got my back, and stands up too, ready for a fight. Then everybody else gets up, revealing their holsters. So much for no weapons in the building. It would be a real Mexican standoff, except that they have guns and we don't have shit anymore. And I know I can practically fly, but bullets are bullets, and these guys have lots of them.

But before I can say something stupid and get us shot, Pete lunges for the window. On his way (cue the super-slo-mo thing again), he grabs the Controller from the table, and me, and we both hurtle through the window, with a million shards of glass (if I never crash through another window again that's just fine with me) and a thousand bullets following us. Peoww! Peoww! Peoww! Peoww! Peoww! Peoww! Peoww! Peoww! Peoww! (I'll stop now. You get the idea.)

PEOWW!
I'm hit.

Fuck! I'm dying! I know it! The pain rips through me, and as we land on the ground (the conference room was like thirty stories up, btw), I'm ready to pass out.

"Don't pass out, dude! Don't pass out! We gotta go!"

But I'm just seeing white dots and shit, and Pete sounds like one of the grown-ups from a Charlie Brown cartoon, and the crazy Peowws are all around us, and I look down and see my pants are turning red – this isn't good.

"Pete… tell Julie… I love her…"

Pete looks down and I can just make out that he's rolling his
eyes at how stupid I am, and I know I'm going to be okay.
"It hit you in the ass, you big baby. Let's go."
He throws me over his shoulders (try that in OUR
dimension, dude!) and leaps off, down past the Lincoln
Memorial, back on to the highway, a half-mile with each
bound, headed for New York.

"They're gonna have attack helicopters and shit after us in
no time. You think we can make the hotel?"
"Not carrying you. And we have to stop and get Meg first."
Meg? Huh? I'm about to say "*But…*" when the look in
Pete's eyes says it all: *No buts.* We are going to get Meg
whether I like it or not. Which I don't.

Pete puts me down on his next leap, and I check my butt.
The bleeding has almost stopped – the bullet really just
grazed me. It still hurts like hell, but it looks totally bad-ass.
("Bad-ass," get it babe?) So I manage to keep up with Pete
the rest of the way to the city, leaving a little rain of blood
droplets for the next three hundred miles. My gift to you,
people of lighter-gravity Earth!

From: Chip Collins
To: Julie Taylor
Date: June 4, 2015 5:43am
Re: About that meteorite…

Hi Julie,

So we're trucking it up to New York at Hulk speed, and practically crash into the Columbia electrical engineering building, running down to the lab where we last saw Meg. She's sitting there soldering something together. Pete catches his breath, reaches into my backpack, rushes over to her, and clunks the device down on the table. Meg's confused.

"What is this?"
"It's an INTERDIMENSIONAL NAVIGATION CONTROLLER."
"Duh. I got that much."
"The government had it. They knew about Tesla all along, but couldn't get through the ITA. They want access through it to find weapons. Weapons! And they've been watching us. We're in danger. You're in danger, too. You have to come with us."
"What? Me? No!"
"Meg, I can't leave you here and let them do God-knows-what to you. I can't."
"No, Pete. Listen. I can handle them. I'll say you threatened me, that I did all this under duress. I'm a smart girl. And I've got clout. I'll figure it out."

"No. You don't understand."
"What's there to understand?"

Pete sits down next to her, cradles her face in his hands.

And kisses her.

Julie, it's maybe the longest kiss I've ever seen. No tongues wagging all over the place, or groaning or groping or anything. But come on, get a room or something.

Then the floor rumbles like an earthquake.

"Wow. That was some kiss, dude."

"That wasn't us, wise-ass. Something's happening outside. Or below us. Meg, what's under us?"
"The Broadway subway line."
"Okay. On the way out, we'll check it out, just to see if anybody needs help. Meg, you get to the hotel."
Pete gets up, grabs the Controller and we start up the stairs. Meg catches up and grabs Pete's sleeve.
"Wait. Before we go."
She reaches up and kisses him. "I'll go with you. For now. But I'm keeping the hundred thousand dollars."
Pete smiles. "We'll negotiate that later. Now get to the hotel. We'll be there in a few minutes."

Out on the street, people are streaming out of the subway station, drenched, screaming about a flood. And sure enough, when me and Pete descend the stairs to the platform, we're completely underwater. There's a subway train about forty feet down the track inside the tunnel, packed with people, trapped.

Now Pete can probably hold his breath for a year, but I'm only good for a minute max, so shit's got to move fast. Pete manages to swim down, squeezing between the tunnel's roof and the top of the subway car.

20 seconds.

He gets to the end of the train and starts pushing. I pull.

30 seconds.

We're pushing a goddamn subway train, all eight cars, down a track. Underwater.

40 seconds.

I'm not gonna make it.

60 seconds.

Holy shit - we get the train into the station. I shoot up the stairs for another gasp of air, then swim back down and crash through the windows (that's right, window-crashing, my new full-time job) and start grabbing people out and getting them to street level as fast as possible.

Finally the last person is out. Now I'm REALLY feeling like a superhero. Saving lives. This is awesome. But time's a wastin', and General Dickhead should be here any minute with his personal attack helicopters and S.W.A.T. teams and shit. So me and Pete shake off and get ready to leave.

And that's when the ground rumbles again.

It's BOK time.

12
The Demon
And The King

From: Chip Collins
To: Julie Taylor
Date: June 4, 2015 5:43am
The Demon and the King

Hi Julie,

So we're standing there, about to be killed by BOK, and I realize the stupid kid's story Meg talked about is REAL. When she first told us we were like, "Blah, blah, blah, Santa Claus, Easter Bunny, whatever. Can we go get some pizza now?" But now that I know the story's not bullshit, I wish I had paid more attention. Not that it would've helped. Because neither one of us has a Magical Sword, so we're screwed.

Wait. Magical Sword – you have no idea what I'm talking about, do you? Okay, while we wait to be killed, here's the full legend:

The Demon and the King
As told by Margaret Thatcher (no relation)
(Interpretation and notes by Chip Collins)

Once upon a time, there was an all-powerful Demon, whose name has long since been forgotten, an enormous monster with a single horn. The very tip of this horn held the Gleaming Stone, a mysterious metal (can you say "chunk of rhodium," kids?) that gave him his powers.

This despicable Demon terrorized the people of the countryside, and kidnapped small children for afternoon snacks. (Obviously this story is told to kids to keep them in line, like *"you better be good goddamnit or the Demon's going to gobble you up!"*)

When the daughter of the King was kidnapped, he swore to avenge her death by ridding the land of the evil Demon forever. Mounting his trusty steed and carrying his Magical Sword (not magical enough to prevent the daughter's kidnapping in the first place? kind of lame if you ask me), he set out to find the Demon in the dark woods.

He found the Demon resting by a river, using the daughter's leg bones as toothpicks (I made that part up, sorry, she was actually still alive in his belly). The King told the Demon he would be dead by sundown, and the Demon laughed. And when he opened his mouth to laugh again, the King could hear his daughter's cries. She was alive! (Really, what are the chances, she would've been dissolved by stomach acid in like three seconds. But it's a legend, so whatever.)

The King had an idea. Knowing that the Demon was vain, he posed a challenge: "Sharper than razors, they say of your teeth. But sharper, I say, is the sword in my sheath."

"Impossible," said the Demon, and he laughed again. So the King drew his Magical Sword, swung it at a small tree, downed it, and sliced it to pieces.

(Pretty bad-ass, I must say.) The Demon, not to be outdone, sunk his head low to the base of a tree and opened his mouth to cut it down. *(Don't do it, Demon! It's a trap!)* At that moment, the King rushed into the Demon's gaping jaws, all the way to his stomach, where his daughter lay near death.

The Demon laughed again at his good luck. But then he felt his stomach rumble. (Spoiler alert: it wasn't gas.) The King sliced open the Demon's belly from the inside, and walked calmly out holding his daughter under his arm! (My father never did shit like that for me. He dropped me off at Laser Tag Kingdom one time. And forgot to pick me up.) And before the Demon could heal its own wound, the King mounted its back, climbed the horn, and cut off the Gleaming Stone, vowing to keep it far away so that the Demon should never return. As the Demon slid into the river, its watery grave, it uttered its last words: "I shall return when the Gleaming Stone is near, whether tomorrow it be, or a thousand year." (Spoiler alert #2: he does return. He's standing right in front of me. Drooling.)

So here he is now, the man (or beast) of the hour, the Demon. BOK. Stupid name, but scary as shit. And he's here to reclaim the Gleaming Stone that me and Pete conveniently delivered right to his riverside grave (hey, nobody told us BOK was buried in the Hudson River, three blocks from Columbia University), near enough for him to rise up, become all-powerful, and terrorize the world again. Whoops. Our bad.

"RUN!!!"

13
We died.
Kidding!

From: Chip Collins
To: Julie Taylor
Date: June 4, 2015 5:43am
We died. Kidding!

Hi Julie,

I'm writing this email, so you know I make it out alive.
But just barely. Here's how:

As we turn to run, BOK's super-long tongue reaches out
and lassos me and Pete (hey, Meg - your stupid story didn't
mention anything about a super-long tongue!). And the
last thing I hear before we're swallowed whole by BOK is
somebody in the crowd: "That's gonna hurt, Awesome Man
and The Brute." That's New Yorkers, just saying shit like it is.

Gulp.

Alone.
Pitch black.
Slimy.
Stinks like a baby's diaper after he eats Gerber Flaming
Curry Chicken Dinner *(now with extra hot sauce!)*

So I'm whimpering (no surprise, I know), while I feel
myself being sucked down to certain death.

But then I feel Pete's hand on my foot, groping around. "Pete!"

I grab his hand, and we squirm until we're face to face.

"Goodbye, dear friend... I shall always-"

"Shut up. Just shut up. God, you have to get better in these situations."

"What? You mean everyday situations like being digested by something out of Monster Week on Channel Eleven?"

Pete smacks me. I deserve it. "Yes. Like this. Listen, we have no time to do this bullshit, we're headed down to the stomach. You ready?"

I'm starting to blubber. "R-ready for what?!"

"Get ready to jump. Right back up. As hard as you can."

I am NOT fucking ready. Who's ready for this shit?

"One..."

I don't even know which way is up!

"Two..."

Hold on! I lost a sneaker!

"Three..."

Wait – are we going on Three, or Go?

"GO!!!"

We both jump. And if we were natives of this dimension, it wouldn't have done shit. We'd still be coasting down to a belly full of death. But we're not from around here. We're built for heavy gravity. Ohhhh yeah.

So we shoot up BOK's throat at a million miles an hour.

KER-SPLATTTT!!!

This is my favorite part: BOK's mouth is closed, so instead of shooting *out*, we shoot *through* – through his skull, smashing it to pieces, and sending BOK brains all over the place. And this thing's brain was huge, so there is literally brain matter covering everything you see for a whole city block. Gross. BOK's lifeless, hulking body drops to the street with a loud, wet THUD. Sucker's dead as a big giant disgusting doornail.

The crowd doesn't know whether to puke – I mean, they're covered in slimy BOK brains – or go back to naming their kids after us for saving their ungrateful asses. They're totally stunned. But after a second, they decide puke it is, and every last one of them is retching on the sidewalk. It's like that joke:

> *What's grosser than gross?*
> *Thousands of people covered in brains*
> *puking on the sidewalk.*

But we're ALIVE, so *Ewww, gross* takes a back seat to *Yay, I'm still breathing.* Pete manages a smile. "That'll teach him to mess with Awesome Man and The Brute." And then he does something I never thought he'd ever do.

He hugs me.

And I can't resist doing my Pete impression. "Get off me. Now."
He grins. "I wouldn't want to be smashing the skull of an ancient giant demon with anybody else, dude."

I'd be wiping away tears this is so sweet, but I'm covered in slime and brains, so I think I'll keep my hands away from my eyes for a little while. And then I hear the attack choppers.

"Uh, dude. Okay, now it's *really* time to go."
Pete nods.
"To the Bat Cave!"
And we're off, leaping, leaving a trail of disgusting goo in our wake.

Thirty seconds later: imagine two brains-covered, herky-jerky-walking, wanna-be superheroes trying to nonchalantly stroll through the lobby of the New Yorker Hotel like it's perfectly normal. Thank God there's no one around. Everyone's outside trying to figure out what the hell is going on.
Uh-oh.
Except some army guy.
He rushes over to us, he's maybe nineteen years old, pistol drawn, all forty pounds of him shaking like a leaf.

"O-On orders of General Arnold, a-and the U.S. Government... y-you two need to come with me."
I point to the TV in the lobby. CNN's showing the disaster area we just left. A scrap of brain drips from the end of my finger.
"Dude. You saw what happened just now, right? Uptown?"
He nods, still shaking.
"And you're seriously going to try to detain us?"
He's not so sure. The gun is drooping.
"How about we just go up to our room, and you say you never saw us? Or... we could just splatter your brains all over the lobby. Either way is fine."
No hesitation. He drops his gun.
"Thanks, dude. Peace out."

We rip up the stairs, and practically run over Meg when we get to Room 3327.

"Yikes. What happened to you two?"
"Long story. Okay, who's got the room key?"
"I do." Pete grabs the doorknob and pulls the whole door off the hinges. (That's five this week. Apparently his job is yanking off doors, and mine is crashing through windows.) We run in. Meg stops.
"Wait."
"No time. Let's go."
Pete shushes me and takes Meg's hand. "What's up?"
"Pete, I just don't know. This is *my* home. Once I step inside, I'll be homeless. Like you. Trying to help you find *your* home, and leaving mine behind. I have a life here."
"You're right. We need you to help us. Help us with the Controller. Help us find Tesla. But I promise, I'll bring you home, when it's safe for you. And…"
Meg stands there, looking in Pete's eyes for the rest.
"And…?"
"…And …I'm afraid if I let you go now, I'll never see you again. I'll never get a chance to see what might have been."
Meg puts her hand over her mouth. A little tear runs down her cheek.

"I'm - I'm sorry. I can't go."

She leans forward and kisses Pete softly on the cheek. Then she retreats, turns away, and walks out the door.

Bummer.

Pete's shell-shocked, but I know better than to make a wise-ass remark right now, and if I try to pat him on the shoulder he'll probably rip my arm off. So we just stand there for a few seconds, listening to Meg's footsteps down the hall.

Then something else.

Gunshots.

Shouting.

Footsteps. Lots of them. Running.

Towards us.

Meg bolts into the room. "Forget everything I just said! I'm coming! HOLD THE DOOR!"

And in the blur of us dodging bullets, running like hell, getting through the ITA, I catch a look at Pete's face.

He's smiling.

14
You're Not Going To Believe This...

From: Chip Collins
To: Julie Taylor
Date: June 4, 2015 5:43am
You're not going to believe this

Hi Julie,

You're not going to believe what I just got...

From: Julie Taylor
To: Chip Collins
Date: June 4, 2015 5:43am
Hi, it's Julie

Hi.

It's Julie.

Julie Taylor.

But there is no Chip Collins, or Pete Turner, so I don't know what the hell you're talking about. And thank God I don't know who you are, because you sound like a douche.

I mean, that's not entirely true. When you're not being a douche, you can be kind of sweet. I hope you find whoever you're looking for.

But whatever, can you stop emailing me?

- Julie

From: Julie Taylor
To: Chip Collins
Date: June 4, 2015 5:43am
Hi, it's Julie again

Hi. It's Julie again.

I just got your last couple of emails. You guys were Awesome Man and The Brute? Jack-ass names, what were you thinking? But defeating BOK? Unreal. You saved the city.

Maybe this Julie girl you're looking for isn't so unlucky after all.

- Julie

From: Chip Collins
To: Julie Taylor
Date: June 4, 2015 5:43am
Re: You're not going to believe this...

Hi Julie,

CRAZY, right? So my guess: when I made that phone call in the lighter gravity dimension, my phone must have started sending out all my emails - to you! But not you-you, Alternate You (scrawny but still beautiful I'm sure). And her replies must've come in just before we got back into the ITA. And there must not be an Alternate Chip or Alternate Pete in her dimension. (Much weirder shit has happened, I don't even ask questions anymore. I just roll with it.)

Now I know it wasn't really you-you, but my heart practically jumped out of my chest when I got those emails. Just the thought of connecting with you, the real you, somehow, across dimensions. And it made me realize something.

This isn't all about me anymore.

Sure, I'd love for you to save me, rescue me from this godforsaken hallway and bring me home. And I want love and attention, and to be babied a little (or a lot). But really? I don't want to come home for me anymore.

I want to come home for YOU.

I want to listen to you. To anticipate your low moments, and show up with chinese take-out and a bottle of wine. To be there when your fish dies and you need me to flush him. To be there when you finish grad school, shouting "take THAT, world!" To make Cancun sunnier, relaxinger, and drunkenner (are those even words?) than you ever imagined. To help you make the ideas that live deep inside you into something real.

Is it stupid of me to imagine us talking?

You put your bag down on the kitchen table after work, and plop down in a chair. "Chip?"
"Whatsup?"
"I'm just feeling down. I don't know why."
"You know what's good for that?"
"Let me guess. Something sex-related."
"No. Ice cream. But it has to be soft-serve, or you'll still feel down. With sprinkles."
"It's February."
"Shhh. That's the secret. The secret to Carvel's Magical Healing Soft-Serve Ice Cream. It only works in February."
And you smile. Maybe for the first time all day.

That's where I want to be.

That's home.

15
Bobo's
New Toy

From: Chip Collins
To: Julie Taylor
Date: June 4, 2015 5:43am
Bobo's new toy

Hi Julie,

So we barely make it into the ITA hallway, after being chased by General Dickhead's thugs, and slamming the ITA door shut (on some poor guy's fingers – you could hear them crunch – sorry, dude).

Whew.

We all let out a little relief laugh, and Pete gives Meg a little *sorry-we-just-ruined-your-life-too* hug, and Bobo comes running over.

"Oh. This is the creature you told me about. He's cute."

Then Bobo starts humping her leg.

"Ick. He *was* cute."
"Whoops. Forgot to tell you about that part. It's his way of saying hi. He likes you."
She shakes Bobo off. "Obviously."

So we scratch a big "MEG" into her dimension's door for reference, and take stock of our resources:

**Chip and Pete's (and now Meg's)
Revised List of Resources:**

1. Bobo (again, not so sure a resource, but we like having him around, and he's funny)

2. ~~One really big plumber's wrench~~

3. ~~One Shogun~~ (General Dickhead took our stuff)

4. One old journal

5. One cell phone

6. One cell phone charger from CVS

7. Three wallets

...*plus new additions*...

8. Meg (questionable resource if you ask me)

9. One INTERDIMENSIONAL NAVIGATION CONTROLLER, basically a heavy shell of rhodium with lots of unexplainable stuff on the inside and a goofy steam-punk-looking display on the outside.

10. Odds and ends: bottle opener (Coronas don't twist off); first-aid kit (good for minor ass wounds); flashlight; safety goggles (whatever, they were a buck at the dollar store); some rope; a couple of Meg's tools from the lab. I have no idea what they do.

11. One backpack to hold everything.

Meg looks puzzled. "What about food?"
"You don't get hungry in here. Time doesn't pass. Weird."
"Right. Then we're ready. Let's start up the Controller and get moving." She toggles the on/off switch.

Nothing.

Toggle. Toggle.

Nothing.

Her hands start shaking.
"Oh my dear lord. This isn't happening."

Pete takes it from her. Toggle, toggle, nothing, toggle,
toggle, nothing, toggle, toggle, nothing. "Fuck. What now?"
"Kick it. That always works in the movies. Sometimes
people even say that exact thing in the movies, about it
working in other movies. Either way, it always works."
Meg grabs the Controller back. "Is that the best you can do,
Chip? Is that how you're planning to survive all this, find
Tesla, and get home? With ill-conceived strategies that rely
on *deus ex machina* to save you?"
"Dayoos ex what?"
"*Deus ex machina.* 'God from the machine.' When you
think a problem can go away by itself, by the hand of fate,
without figuring it out yourself."
"Blah, blah, whatever. Try it."
So just to disprove me, she puts the Controller down
gently on the floor, and gives it a little shove with her foot.
Nothing.
"See? Now can we move on to a more productive
troubleshooting strategy?"
I walk right past her and punt the controller at Bobo. It
hits him in the chest and bounces into the air. He fumbles
around, hands waving, and catches it just before it hits the
ground.

The Controller lights up and starts humming.

Bobo's thrilled with his new toy, and starts the Bobo dance.
I turn to Meg. "You're welcome."
She gives me the finger.
"Huh. I didn't think they gave the finger in your
dimension."
"They don't. Pete showed me how to do it." She smiles at
Pete.
"Awww, how cute." And I give them both the finger. So
now we're all standing there giving each other the finger,
and Bobo must think it's some kind of friendship sign or
something, so he puts down the Controller and tries it too.
But he's got the wrong number of fingers, like two fingers
and a thumb, so it looks wrong. But he makes due, and
gives us all his weird Bobo finger, and it's hilarious, so we
start laughing, and Bobo raises his hands even higher and
starts his dance again. Man, sometimes I think Bobo's the
only one who's got it all figured out, like "fuck everything -
let's dance!"
Anyway, we get the Controller working, and Meg replaces
the dorky old-fashioned screen thing on top with the cool
smartphone version she came up with, and she looks proud
of herself.
"Not Controller. *INController.*"
"Huh?"
"That's what we should call it. Short for Interdimensional
Navigation Controller. And it puts you in control. Sort of.
Get it? INController."
"Great. Whatever. Do you get a fee for naming it, too?"
Meg gives me the finger again.
"Wow, you're really getting the hang of that."

Pete walks over and lowers her hand. "You might not want to overuse that. It's more for special occasions. Just ignore ninety percent of what Chip says and you'll be fine."
I'm hurt. "Really? So that's how it's going to be?"
"Come on, dude. It took me like two years to get used to you in college. I have to get Meg up to speed faster. Give her a break."
Whatever. I'll consider it. I mean, I do talk shit constantly, so he's got a point. And we need her. Sort of. So I hand her the journal, open to the entry with Tesla's location, and she taps it into the INController (and I have to give her credit - it's a kick-ass gadget name). Then she stops and looks at us.

"Wait a second."
"What?"
"I just want to state the obvious, before we proceed."
"What? What's so obvious?"
"You now have an INController."
"Yeah. Duh. And?"
"And you have the coordinates for your home dimension."
"Yeah. And?"
"So if you're trying to get home, why do you need Tesla?"

16
To Tesla,
Or Not To Tesla

From: Chip Collins
To: Julie Taylor
Date: June 4, 2015 5:43am
To Tesla, or not to Tesla

Hi Julie,

Hmmm.

We really never even thought about it. But Meg's totally right, as usual. I think we just assumed we needed Tesla to get home, but the tools are right there in our hands.

We don't need to risk our asses to rescue Tesla.
We can go home. NOW.
Should we?

And Julie, I'd like to say that it's an easy decision, like "Fuck no, we're heroes! Of course we're going to save Tesla first!" But really, we're just a couple of guys, tired and beat up, and desperate for a nice, long shower and a few minutes of normal. We didn't get into this to save anybody. And Tesla got himself into this shit, didn't he? Why should it be on us to bail him out?

"Hey Pete, whatcha thinking?"
"I don't know, dude. I mean, I know the right thing to do, but…"

"But your whole body is telling you to press the big UNDO button and get the hell out of here?"

"Exactly. It's hard to resist. If you asked me a week ago there wouldn't even be a question. But now, I don't know."

Meg walks over to Pete, puts her hand on his arm. "I'm not saying one way or the other, it's your choice, but know that you don't owe Nikola Tesla anything."

Me and Pete stare at each other for a while, we're both waiting for the other to make the decision. I'm dreaming about you and me eating waffles in bed as the sun peeks into our bedroom window. Pete's probably thinking about taking Meg to a nice dinner at Prego. Neither one of us is dreaming about the glory of dying to save our friend Nikola.

Fuck. This is terrible.
Home.
Tesla.
Waffles.
Guilt.
Sunrise.
Shame.
A warm shower.
An old inventor.
Someone in need.
Fuck.

I break first. "Damnit. Well, he better be overjoyed to see us."

Pete smiles. "Good choice, dude. I guess Tesla beats waffles."

"Hey, how the fuck did you know I was thinking about waffles?"

"Dude, I've known you for a long time. That's your go-to fantasy."

"Were you thinking about Pregos?"

He pats me on the shoulder. "No. Birthday cake."

Meg claps her hand onto the journal. "Okay, while this is sweet, now that we've reached a decision, we should start right away. Chip, I assume at some point you asked Tesla about this prison he's in?"

"No."

"Or who's holding him there?"

"No."

"Or why he's being held?"

"No."

"Were you going to ask?"

"No."

"May I ask why?"

"No. Whatever. Just give me back the damn book."

So I write back to Tesla, and Julie, this is our actual conversation. I couldn't make this shit up if I tried.

"Nikola – who is holding you captive?"

"Astonishing! Chip, how could you possibly know that?"

"Know what?"

"Who is holding me captive!"

"It was a question, not an answer."

"I don't understand."

"Again – who is holding you captive?"

"Yes."

"No, not yes. I was asking their name."

"Who."

"Whoever is holding you captive."

"Not whoever, who."

"Nikola, this isn't the time to be correcting my grammar. Answer the question."

"I did. Who is holding me captive."

"Yes. The name please."

"The name is Who."

Ahhhh! Finally, I get it. The bad guy's name is "Who!" I almost got stuck in an infinite *Abbott and Costello* loop there with Tesla.

"So let me get this straight – the guy that's holding you prisoner is named 'Who.'"

"I'm not sure it is even a 'guy,' but 'Who' is the best I can ascertain. When I ask him 'Who are you?' he simply replies 'Who am I? WHO AM I?' And laughs. In fact, that is the entirety of our conversations. Rather boring fellow."

"Okay. Now what about the prison? I have the location, but what is it like?"

"It is at the end of the hallway."

"Wait. The end? There is no end."

"That is what I thought. But WHO – I shall use capital letters to clarify the use of his name – has somehow created an end. I now fear the worst."

"Great. I thought we had done 'worst.' Several times already. What could possibly be the new worst?"

"Chip, the multiverse is composed of all the infinite possible universes. Every possibility, at every moment in time, becomes its own very real, very beautiful universe, interconnected but separate, like the fibers of a cloth. The hallway and the doors of the ITA provide a way to move from one to the other. The only way an end of the hallway could exist is..."

"...If the universes behind the doors were destroyed. If the possibilities were eliminated."

"Correct, Chip. I hesitate to tell you how far reaching... well, let me simply say that I hope my theory is wrong. You must move very quickly now, Chip. We may not have the time I originally thought. We may be facing the end of..."

"Of...? Of what?"

"The end of the multiverse. The end of... everything."

Woah. Mind-fuck. Did he just say everything? What the hell does that even mean? Like I'm going to die? We're all going to die? Wait – Julie – you're going to die?

My hands start shaking, and I can't even write back to Tesla. Not that there's any reason to. I already know the answer to any question I might have: if we don't get Tesla the hell out of there soon, we're all going to die.

From: Chip Collins
To: Julie Taylor
Date: June 4, 2015 5:43am
Re: To Tesla, or not to Tesla

Hi Julie,

I can't move. Sure, I've had several near-death experiences already, but having Tesla spell out the end of everything for me? The end of you? Of us? I am literally petrified.

What would you say to me right now? I know. The same thing you said when I was scared to go into the haunted house that time. You'd say "Suck it up, Chip. It's a church carnival haunted house for Pete's sake, the whole thing fits on a flatbed, and there aren't even any real people in there to scare you, you baby!" And you pushed me in and I was fine. (After I screamed a couple of times.)

So I swallow hard, and suck it up, and decide to keep my mouth shut. No sense freaking Pete and Meg out, too. I take a step. And another. And another. My legs are slowly unfreezing.
"Nice zombie walk, dude. You mind telling us what the fuck is going on?"
"Nothing. Nothing. It's all good. The prison should be a piece of cake. Here are the coordinates."
I hand Meg the journal open to the coordinates (59380918.593820e+482024.id.mt if you're counting).
She punches them in, and the INController starts doing its

thing (whatever the hell that is). Then *Breep!* Just like a GPS, it highlights a path (no spoken directions though – maybe there's an app for that) more or less directly to Tesla.

After a few hours (days? weeks?) of walking, the thing Breeps! again. Stop. Enter the door on your left. So we put Bobo (our professional tester) in the doorway just in case, and Pete unlocks it. Psshhh. Bobo doesn't get snatched, or eaten, or blown up, so we take a peek.

It's an elevator.

"An elevator?"
"Remember our new motto, dude: *'Shit's crazy. Don't ask.'*"
"Wait. I thought it was *'Find Tesla. Go Home.'*"
"No. That was our old motto. The new motto is *'Shit's crazy. Don't ask.'*"
"Got it. Well, if I had to guess, I'd say this is one of the shortcuts Tesla was talking about. Okay, you first."
"No dude, be my guest."
"How about ladies first?"
Meg pipes up. "Bobo wants to go first, don't you boy?" She nudges Bobo into the elevator. No plummeting to death? Good. Everybody gets in. The door closes.

"Wait. No buttons?"

Immediately the elevator plummets at a zillion miles an hour. We're all pushed to the ceiling, screaming (except for Bobo, who's digging this).

AAAAAAAAAHHHHHHHH!!!
AAAAAAAAAHHHHHHHH!!!

AAAAAAAAAHHHHHHHH!!!
AAAAAAAAAHHHHHHHH!!!
AAAAAAAAAHHHHHHHH!!!
AAAAAAAAAHHHHHHHH!!!
AAAAAAAAAHHHHHHHH!!!

I yell to Pete over the screaming of the elevator car cables,
"I'M SORRY!"
"FOR WHAT?"
"FOR NOT TELLING YOU WE'RE ALL GOING TO DIE!"

And on cue, the elevator slows to a gentle halt.

We slide to the floor. Silence.

"For not telling me WHAT?!"
So much for sucking it up and keeping my mouth shut.
"Listen, dude. It's bad. If we don't get to Tesla soon, some
nasty shit is going to happen. Something big is unravelling.
Like multiverse big. And fast."
I'm trembling a little I guess, because Pete grabs my
shoulders and steadies me. He smiles. "Well, then I guess
we'll have to take a faster elevator from now on, not this slow
piece of shit." And I smile back. And again Pete has made the
end of it all so much better. I exhale. Thanks, dude.

Meg stands up first. "So does the door just ope-"

Ding!

The door opens.

This is NOT a shortcut.

17
I Finally Went To Church (Sort Of)

From: Chip Collins
To: Julie Taylor
Date: June 4, 2015 5:43am
I finally went to church (sort of)

Hi Julie,

The elevator door opens, and it's really dark. And quiet.
And musty. Incense burning. As our eyes adjust to the lack
of light, we can make out the inside of a church, or temple
or something. Tapestries and candles hanging on the walls.
Right in front of us is a huge altar. And beyond that, the
floor…

…is moving?

Wait. It's not the floor. There's something covering the floor,
alive.

Hold it together, Chip. Don't shit in your pants, Chip.

It's people. Or something. Very orange. They're prostrating
themselves, bowing low toward the altar and us.

Then they slowly rise. Probably a hundred and fifty of
them. Their eyes are all whites. And glowing. They're
moving toward us.

"HOLY SHIT!! SORRY, WRONG FLOOR!! DOOR CLOSE!!
DOOR CLOSE!! GOING UP!!"

We're pounding all over the walls of the elevator, hoping
we're pressing some invisible buttons. Meg must hit the
right spot because the door starts to close.

But just like real life, some idiot sticks his hand in and
stops the door from closing at the last second. I try to push
the orange hand back out to let the door close, but it's too
late. The door opens back up. A bright orange dude with a
diaper on and white glowing eyes is standing six inches in
front of us. I whisper to Pete. "Okay, NOW we're all going
to die."

Click. Clack. Click. Cuk-cuk.

Huh? What's making that annoying sound?

Click. Clack. Click. Cuk-cuk.

Wait. It's Orange Dude. He's making the sound with his
mouth. Just standing there. Not moving, just clicking away.
Like he's waiting for a response.
"Meg, you're the smart one. Tell him we're lost."
"N-n-n-n-n-..."
She's freaking out. I guess she's not used to crazy shit
happening every five seconds. So Pete takes the lead. "We
are humans. From another dimension. We mean you no
harm." Orange Dude squints at Pete.

Click. Clack. Click. Cuk-cuk.

"Whatever. Your turn, dude."

I clear my throat. "Clickety-friends! Clackety-peace-be-with-you. Cluck-cluck, click." I'm smiling as broad as I can and nodding while Pete rolls his eyes. But Orange Dude is mimicking my smile and my nod. I whisper again to Pete, "It's working!"
So I figure let's get the hell out of here while the gettin's good. "Okay, so we'll be clickety-going now, clackety-bye-bye. Thanks for the clickety-warm welcome, folks." I motion to Meg and she slowly presses the invisible door-close button. The door starts to close.

CLACK!! CLACK!! CLACK!!

Uh-oh. Orange Dude is not happy. He draws a knife from the back of his diaper, pulls opens the door again, points the tip of his knife right at my eye, and motions for me to exit the elevator.

Cuk-cuk! Click. Clack. Click. Cuk-cuk!

We all shuffle out of the elevator r-e-a-l s-l-o-w. And as soon as Meg passes the doorway, she crumples and falls.
"Meg!" Pete rushes to her, and about ten orange dudes pull their knives and surround him and go to grab her. But they don't know Pete.
"STOP!!"
The dudes freeze in their tracks. "She's weak. Her body's not used to this gravity. I'll carry her. BACK OFF." And Julie, Pete talks the universal language when he's like this – they totally get him and back off.

**BTW, My Really Official Explanation
on the Meg Thing:**
Meg was fine in her own gravity. And fine in the
ITA, walking and lifting things no problem. So I'm
thinking the ITA somehow allows you to travel
the hallway as if it were your own environment.
Gravity, air, light, whatever, it adapts to your sense
of normal. *(Normal! Ha!)* But in another dimension,
you're at that environment's mercy. Pete liked this
explanation, and told me maybe I'm not such an
idiot after all.

Pete picks up Meg, and Orange Dude herds us all around
the front of the altar, to another round area with a low
circular table in the middle. More of the orange dudes,
knives drawn, sit us on benches at the edge of the round
area, and prepare some chains.

This isn't going to happen if I can help it. As they start
to chain our ankles to the table pedestal, I slowly get my
hand into my backpack and fumble for the Shogun. Fuck.
General Dickhead took it. Okay, Plan B. I make a quick nod
to Pete. He nods back.

"GO!!"

We bolt for the elevator, him carrying Meg and me carrying
Bobo, ripping free of the dudes trying to hold us.

We're gonna make it!

From: Chip Collins
To: Julie Taylor
Date: June 4, 2015 5:43am
Re: I finally went to church (sort of)

Hi Julie,

Well, we don't make it. Eight orange dudes block the elevator door, knives drawn. Pete tries to barrel through, but it's no use – there's just too many of them, and they're too strong, even for Pete. They pile on (why don't they just kill us? we don't even wind up with a scratch), drag us back over to the benches, and chain us up good. We can move around a few feet, but we ain't going very far now. I glare at Orange Dude.

"Hey, you! So what the fuck do you want?"

Click. Clack. Click. Cuk-cuk.

He points to three painted images on the floor, surrounding the table:

> Image 1: Three figures walking through a doorway, with a bunch of clouds and shit around it. There are orange dudes wailing, very afraid.
>
> Image 2: One of the figures is bent over a low table, beheaded. (Oh shit, I'm starting to see where this is going.)
>
> Image 3: The same figure, head magically

reattached, now glowing and floating and smiling. All the orange dudes are praising him and dancing.

"Uh, Meg. I don't like the look of this. Your take?"
She's still weak, but looking more like normal over-confident Meg now. "I believe whoever walks through that doorway must offer a sacrifice. If the person sacrificed is able to resurrect from the dead, he is proven to be their messiah. My guess."
"But we can't do that! My head doesn't go back on like that!"
"You didn't ask me for a happy ending. You just asked what it meant."
"Next time remind me to ask for a happy ending instead."

Pete shuffles in his ankle chains right up to Orange Dude's face. He's making all kinds of hand gestures, pointing, etc. Lots of clicking and nodding going on. He shuffles back over to me and Meg. "I think if one of us takes the test and fails, which we will, the sacrifice is complete, and the others are set free. I think. They don't seem to be wanting to kill us all, I think they just want their messiah. I'll do it."
Me and Meg both protest.

"No. I'll do it." "No. I'll do it."

I'm not letting him be the hero again. "Come on, Pete. Look at the situation. You finally found someone for you that's actually smart. She needs you and you need her. And we all know that the odds are slim that I'll ever see Julie again. And I got you into this shit to begin with. And if there's anyone better equipped to rescue Tesla and figure this whole thing out, it's you. You and Meg."

Pete's shaking his head. "Don't be stupid. I have to-"

I grab his arm. "PLEASE, dude. You have been my courage this whole time. You've covered my ass for years. Let me cover yours. Let me pay you back. Once. You deserve it. Please. Besides, it's your birthday."

Pete laughs, but he's got the beginning of a tear in his eye. And Meg's got one running down her cheek. I reach down and wipe hers away.

"Meg, I was just giving you shit because I was jealous. You're a peach. Take care of my friend here. He's the best." Pete leans down too, and we all share a little hug.

"Oh, by the way, I've been meaning to tell you, dude – you know how you could never figure out what happened to your signed Derek Jeter baseball? Well me and Julie were having a catch with it, and it kind of went out the window. We tried to run downstairs to get it back, but a dog ran off with it. So, mystery solved, right?"

"Just shut up, dude." And he hugs me a little tighter.

Orange Dude breaks up our sweet little goodbye, and I raise my hand. He leads me over to the table, and bends me down, so my face is touching the stone. God, would it kill them to heat this thing up a little? It's freaking cold!

I can see out of the corner of my eye, a bigger one of these guys raising a pretty bad-ass sword. He brings it down slow, to make sure he's got the right angle on my neck. He raises it again. I close my eyes.

Julie, please forgive me. I really did love you.

From: Chip Collins
To: Julie Taylor
Date: June 4, 2015 5:43am
Re: I finally went to church (sort of)

Hi Julie,

Holy shit. So I'm about to be beheaded, with zero chance of being the stupid messiah these idiots are hoping for. Sorry to dash your hopes, morons.

My eyes are closed shut, waiting for impact.

Then I feel something else.

Fur.

Bobo. He's on me. What the fuck?

I open my eyes. Bobo is laying on top of me, blocking the guy with the sword. So the guy tries pushing him off with his foot, clicking and clacking at Bobo. But he's not budging. Bobo leans his face down to mine, so our eyes are literally an inch from each other, and for the first time, I really see them. They're huge. His eyes go on forever, and there's a message coming out of them:

I DO THIS.

"No."

I DO THIS.

"I said no."

TRUST.

Huh? Am I going crazy? I'm talking to myself! Get the fuck off me, Bobo! Pete and Meg are yelling, but I only see their mouths moving. I can't hear anything. I'm dizzy. Bobo pushes me to the ground, off the table. Puts his face to the stone.

I stumble to my feet. But before any of us can rush to stop it, the sword comes down on Bobo's neck.

He's gone.

Bobo's dead.

From: Chip Collins
To: Julie Taylor
Date: June 4, 2015 5:43am
Re: I finally went to church (sort of)

Hi Julie,

Bobo? Little buddy? I jump on Orange Dude and start beating on him. "YOU KILLED MY FRIEND, YOU ORANGE SON OF A BITCH!!!" And he's letting me go to town, punching him in the face, and he's not lifting a finger. He puts his knife away, and kneels down. Pete finally pulls me off him, and Julie – the dude is crying. Not because I'm hurting him (I'm not), but because it didn't work. He didn't get his messiah.

He killed Bobo and didn't get his messiah. Now they're all moaning and wailing.

"Good. That's what you get for killing him, you stupid fucks! Cry your eyes out!"

And poor Bobo's laying there in pieces. Goddamnit. I mean, I know we put him directly in harm's way a lot, and I didn't even think about it because he's pretty much indestructible, but I never really thought he'd actually DIE. Bobo doesn't die, right?

And he didn't deserve it. He was always happy. And loyal. And in the end, he was the one who put it on the line for the rest of us. What a stand-up guy. A hero.

So of course now I'm weeping over his dead body, and Meg comes over and whispers to me, "You were about to do the same thing for Pete. That was the bravest thing I've ever seen." And she kisses me on the cheek. And that just makes it harder, because I didn't get to make it right with Pete – in fact, I'm pretty much responsible for all the misery he's going through. We're all going through. Fuck. Poor Bobo. I'm really sorry, dude. Can you forgive me too?

Meanwhile, Pete's been hand-waving and nodding with Orange Dude (that total dick), and I guess confirms that we're free to go. The sacrifice has been made. But we stick around while they wrap Bobo up in a shroud, like a little mummy. It's kind of cute (I can't believe I just said that, but it's true). They take him to the back of this temple, and there's a big wall of drawers, like a mausoleum.

They lay him onto an open drawer, and chant something in their click language (mental note: I now know the answer to the question 'what is the most annoying sound in the universe?'). I'm covering my ears, and sniffing back tears, we're all pretty broken up. Orange Dude slides the drawer shut. Boom. Done.

They release our chains, and the three of us shuffle back towards the elevator. We walk inside, turn around, and in perfect unison – give them the finger.

Meg says, "It's a special occasion."

The orange dudes look blankly at our gesture. The door closes.

"This sucks."

Meg puts her hand on my shoulder. "Yes, Chip, it does. But you said yourself, we have very little time, so we'll have to mourn later. Let's honor Bobo by getting to Tesla before it's too late." She turns around and around, looking up and down. "There must be some way to control this elevator... here!"

On the back wall, there's a little indentation. Barely noticeable. But just the right shape to fit the bottom pluggy-looking thing on the INController.

"Bingo." Pete places it onto the indentation, and immediately the INController starts humming and lighting up.

"Okay, it's got this dimension's data. We were only off by a few million. Which, in terms of infinity, is pretty close. Let's recalculate the route." Meg presses some buttons, and the elevator sounds like it's starting to gear back up to a zillion miles an hour.

"Wait. What was that?"
"What, dude?"
"A knock. On the door."
"No. We're moving, that's all."

And then the elevator rocks into gear, and zigs and zags all over the place, at break-neck speed for a solid minute (hour? year?), until I feel my stomach emptying itself into my mouth. But I hold it back, and thank God it comes to an end. The elevator stops. Ding! The door opens. Another hallway.

"Okay, we're getting closer, dude. A few more shortcuts, and we'll be there. You want to write to Tesla and let him know about our daring rescue mission?"

"No. Wait."

"Wait what."

"Just wait. Give me a second." They're now both standing in the hallway, but I'm still in the elevator. Pete's tapping his fingers. Meg's tapping her foot.

"Listen, something's not right. There was a knock at the door back there."

"No there wasn't. It was the elevator moving."

"How do you know? You an ITA elevator technician now?"

"Dude. I know you're upset about Bobo. We all are. But we have to move forward. You told us we didn't have a lot of time. And we're standing here wasting more right now."

"I know, I know. Sorry. But we have to go back."

"WHAT? No."

"I'm going. I know it doesn't make sense. It's only a few minutes."

"That could've been a week, dude. You know how it is in here. Get out of that elevator and let's go."

Julie, I don't know what I'm thinking, but I grab the INController out of Pete's hands, shut the elevator door, slam the INController into place and hit the "back" button on the smartphone interface.

I'm now alone, zig-zagging across the damn multiverse, almost throwing up, I've left Pete and Meg, the two smart ones, behind, and I'm probably going to step through that door and have to sacrifice myself all over again just because I thought I heard a knock on a door.

I am a total idiot.

From: Chip Collins
To: Julie Taylor
Date: June 4, 2015 5:43am
Re: I finally went to church (sort of)

Hi Julie,

The elevator comes to a stop. And as soon as the door opens partway, a hand grabs my arm.

CLACK CLACK CLACK CLACK!!!

Yup, that's it. I'm dead. I am going to be beheaded because I came through the doorway. Damn. And I've been pretty good at decision-making lately. Oh well. At least me and Bobo can be next door neighbors in their mausoleum.

But the hand isn't leading me to the circular table, it's pulling me quickly around it to the back room, right to the wall of drawers. It's Orange Dude. He points to Bobo's drawer. All the other orange dudes have surrounded it and are standing there, frozen.

Clack! Cuk! Cuk!

The drawer is moving a little bit.

"What are you waiting for, schmucks? Open up the damn drawer!"

They don't move, so I lunge at the drawer and throw it open.

The little mummy shape is definitely moving. *Ewww.*

But not like waving its hands or anything. More like morphing. It's like undulating under the surface. And growing. It's sort of disgusting, really disgusting, to watch. I'm afraid Bobo's poor body is not going down quietly. It's going to explode all over us or something, like BOK brains.

We all back up a few steps.

Whatever's going on under those bandages is stretching them to the breaking point. Stretching, stretching. Man, it's going to go any second. What the hell am I doing here?

SSSSKKKRRRAAAALLLLCCCHHH!

(That's the closest I can get to typing the sound is makes when the bandages burst and dissolve into a million pieces.)

Holy shit.

It's Bobo.

And there are two of him.

He's back!

From the dead! And there's two of him! Identical Bobos! I am so freaked out by how weird this is, but even happier to see him/them, so I run up to one of them, get really close to his eyes, look deep into them. I'm like "hello in there, dude! Got anything to say, buddy?"

Blink. Blink.

"Really? Nothing?"

Blink. Blink.

Oh well. I guess I was going crazy when I thought he was talking to me on the chopping block. But man am I thrilled! I give them both a big hug, and they start doing a little jig, perfectly together, like mirror images. More weird. But who cares? He's/They're ALIVE!!!

And then the orange dudes, after getting over their initial shock, fall to the ground and start waving their bodies up and down in prayer, toward the two Bobos. And it hits me:

Bobo is their messiah.

He rose from the dead.

How cool is that? Bobo's a GOD! So I'm like "hey Bobo, maybe you should do some god-like stuff, give them a message of love and peace or some shit. Go ahead."

Blink. Blink. (Times two.)

And then they give the orange dudes the Bobo finger.

Hmmm. Probably not what these guys were expecting. They're looking for love and harmony and guidance and you guys give them the finger. But to you it's a friendship sign, right? So maybe it'll be the friendly greeting of all orange dudes for the next thousand millennia. Nice. I approve.

"Okay, guys. So you going to stick around and be gods – which is totally cool, I wouldn't blame you – or are you coming with me and Pete?"

They definitely understand the word Pete, because they both jump into my arms, so now I look like that guy who won two big stuffed animals at the carnival. Okay, I guess it's *be gods* later, *save Tesla* now. So while they orange dudes are still in their praying ecstasy, we mosey on over to the elevator.

We get in, and right before the elevator door shuts, as the orange dudes raise their ecstatic faces to the Bobos for some divine guidance or something, there's a word. Like the two Bobos are saying it together, but not in spoken words, more like in a little combined thought bubble over their heads. Just one word:

PEACE.

18
Shit Just Got
(Even More) Real

From: Chip Collins
To: Julie Taylor
Date: June 4, 2015 5:43am
Shit just got (even more) real

Hi Julie,

Ding!

The door opens, and Pete's right there in front of me.

And he punches me in the face.

Ouch. That's the second time. I go down.

"What the hell were you thinking, dude? This isn't the *Chip-Does-Whatever-The-Fuck-He-Wants* Show!! That kind of stupid shit could get us all killed! AND you lost my fucking Derek Jeter baseball. It was signed, man. So what do you have to say for yourse-"

And the two Bobos rush out and start humping his legs. Pete releases his fists and laughs, and starts petting them.

"What the fuck?"

"He died. And he came back! Weird. He's their messiah, dude, it's hilarious."
Pete points to Bobo Two. "Where'd the other one come from?"

"Yeah, that's the weird part. They both came out of the same mummy bandages."

Meg laughs. "Asexual reproduction."

"Uh, come again?"

"Asexual reproduction. It has to be. In this case, of the fragmentation type – like a starfish. See, when you cut a starfish in half, each half grows back into a whole, and the result is two complete starfish. So he didn't actually die. He probably went into a state of shock when he was beheaded, and then after the shock wore off, began regenerating his tissue. Fascinating."

"Whatever. Thanks for the explanation, Spock."

"Who's Spock?"

"Never mind. Hey, you want your leg humped? There's enough Bobos to go around."

"No, thank you. I'll enjoy it from a distance."

Pete's right back to business. "Okay, gang's back together. Plus one extra Bobo. Hooray. Now here are the new rules:"

"Pete's New Rules:

1. Nobody leaves the group. Chip did it because he's an idiot, but he brought the Bobos back, so he's forgiven. But not again. We need to stick together if we're going to get Tesla.

2. I'll handle the INController. If you try to take it, I will cut your hand off.

3. Speaking of cutting hands off, nobody cut anything off Bobo. We already have two of him, and even though we like him, we don't need any more Bobos.

4. And the most important rule is…"

A rumble rocks the hallway.

"What? What's the most important rule?"
"Shhhh! Shut the fuck up!"
"Is that the rule, or are you just telling me to shut the fuck up?"
"Right now it's the new most important rule! Shut the fuck up and listen!"

So we listen. Nothing.

Then another rumble.

Then searing pain. We all fall to the floor, doing whatever we can do to squirm away from it. It's like somebody's ripping out a slice of you, right from the good, juicy, middle part. Julie, I'm sorry to say this, but the only thought I'm having is: *kill me and end this.* That's how bad it is.

And then it's over. Just like that. No after effects at all. Gone. Like, did it even really happen?

"Nikola – what the hell was that?"

"Dear Chip,
You are close enough to me now where you can feel the results of a universe collapse. My theory was correct. WHO has indeed learned how to reduce the number of possibilities in the multiverse. They are no longer infinite. And he is using the ITA to collapse universes one-by-one.

What you felt was one of your very own possibilities being erased. I felt it too, as I have several before. They are quickening.

I do not know WHO's ultimate goal. But he must be stopped. It is no longer important simply to retrieve me. We must stop WHO."

Great. My to-do list just got longer:

Chip's To-Do List:

1. Rescue Tesla.

• • • **NEW: 1b – Stop WHO and Save the Multiverse.** • • •

2. Shoot back to dimension #234,698,594,394,683

3. Heat up that lasagna.

4. Get married (to you, schnookums).

5. Live happily ever after.

Save the multiverse. I mean, if I wasn't in such a rush to get back, and to start living our best years together, it might even sound cool to do that. "Save the multiverse." But I don't want to be a hero. It was a nice place to visit. But I've already had enough adventures for infinite lifetimes. I'm not looking forward to it. You know the part I look forward to every day?

This.

Writing these emails to you. I don't need super powers or magical swords. I just like connecting with you, even if it's an imaginary connection, for a little while every day. I feel like I keep taking little steps closer to you, even if you can't write back. And it's not the desperate writing of a madman, these emails, not just something to keep me sane. It's me, holding the little fire of something we might have together, protecting that little ball of fire, carrying it, feeding it twigs, growing it a little each day, making sure it's got enough air.

And now, I've got to do something actually important, for the first time in my life. Something important for all of us. But the only thing I really want to do is keep that fire going, keep Chip and Julie alive in my dreams. Is that selfish?

19
Why Did I Think Tesla Would Still Look Forty?

From: Chip Collins
To: Julie Taylor
Date: June 4, 2015 5:43am
Why did I think Tesla would still look forty?

Hi Julie,

We're really close now. Have we been traveling the ITA
for weeks? Months? Years? It's impossible to tell. I tried
counting my emails to you, three a day maybe? One a
week? Phooey. We've taken a few shortcuts, had some more
near-death experiences (no surprise. Btw, I'm going to write
a book about this at some point when I get back.) But we're
feeling the rumbles and the pain more frequently now, and
the INController is tracking our path.

We're here.

There. Up ahead. Something.
"Hmm. What do you make of it, dude?"
"Are you serious?"
He's right. How do you make anything of what we're
seeing? It looks like the hallway, but also the opposite of the
hallway. Whatever that is. Like the hallway takes a bunch
of turns in all directions, but they all end in the same place,
right where we're looking. Trust me, it's freaky.

Tesla has told us WHO isn't around. He comes and goes,
collapsing a universe here, collapsing a universe there,

and I guess taking a cigarette break in between, maybe going down to the Bahamas for a breather. We still don't know shit about him, and that scares the hell out of all of us, including Tesla. Who is he? Why is he doing this? Does he realize what an asshole name WHO is?

We get closer to the beginning of the area we're calling the prison. It definitely has that look like if you touch it it'll disappear. Same hallway, we can walk down it, but a little more like walking into a bouncy castle. Just a little. And hard to focus on.

"*Breep!* You have arrived at your destination. The door is to your right." (Meg's been tweaking the INController, so now we've got spoken turn-by-turn directions. She rocks.)

We turn to the door and review our plan:

The Plan:

Step 1. I tie our rope around my waist, a la *Poltergeist*, and enter the doorway.

Step 2. Pete holds on tight and never lets go, or I'm going to be lost forever, and really pissed at him.

Step 3. I find Tesla through one of the doors on the other side. Wow that sounds so easy. I like this step.

Step 4. Pete pulls us out. We run like hell.

Step 5. Figure out how to stop WHO (admittedly, our least planned-out step)

Now, all of this assumes that WHO doesn't stroll by right in the middle of our plan and go "hey, who the fuck are you?", and Pete can pull us both out, and that it's not a trap or anything.

So we get all set, and I'm about to step into the doorway.
"Dude. You never told me. What was the most important rule?"
He grins. "It was 'Don't Ask Questions.' So shut up and get the hell in there."
I go to step in, and Bobo (not sure which one) jumps on me.
"C'mon, Bobo. This isn't the time for dicking around."
He holds on to me a little tighter. He's not letting go. Meg's lightbulb pops on again. "You know, Chip, Bobo might have an idea. If somehow he shares his brain activity with Bobo Two – as evidenced by the fact that they have perfectly synchronized movement – that may be an asset in navigating through the prison and back out. Pete, what do you think?"
"I think it's another thirty pounds."
Pete tries to pry Bobo off, but he's locked on to me pretty tight at this point. So instead, Pete unceremoniously pushes us both through the doorway. "Whatever."

So I'm expecting to fall through some *Twilight Zone* door, spiraling for a few minutes through space while the credits roll, screaming the whole time:

AAAAAAAAGGGHGGHGHGHGH
AAAAAAAAGGGHGGHGHGHGH
AAAAAAAAGGGHGGHGHGHGH
AAAAAAAAGGGHGGHGHGHGH
AAAAAAAAGGGHGGHGHGHGH
AAAAAAAAGGGHGGHGHGHGH!!!

But instead, it's literally like walking through a doorway. It takes three milliseconds. So my scream is like:

AA-

That's it? Wow, that wasn't so bad.

I tug on the rope. Pete tugs back. Check.
I look into Bobo's eyes. Blink. Blink. Check.
Okay, now where the hell is Tesla? I start walking the hallway, turning corners, retracing my steps, taking a different hallway, (I won't bore you with the details but it was basically an hour or so of this) and…

Bump.

I bump into Nikola Tesla.

We did it.
We found Tesla!

I tug on the rope three times to let Pete know. (I came up with that code – pretty fancy, right?) Pete tugs back three times. We're already at Step 3 of our plan. Cool. And then I really get a good look at Tesla for the first time.

I'll admit, after all this, I expected the heavens to open up and a choir of angels to shout "You've arrived!", and rainbows and unicorns and shit would be popping out, and Tesla would be in long flowing robes made out of rhodium, and he'd say something like "Chip, you have earned the status of Highest Order of the Heroes! Welcome!"

But none of that shit happens.

Tesla's just standing there in his gray suit from the forties
(it's a nice suit, it probably cost a year's salary back then,
but still it's no robe made out of rhodium). And man, is he
OOOOOLLLLLLDDDDD. Like any pictures I saw of him
were from his handsome forties, I guess. I keep forgetting
he walked into the ITA when he was 86. But the good news
is he's like a tall, regal old, like my sinewy old grandpa who
was 6'3" and used to jump into frozen lakes in January.
And his eyes are full of energy, like mini-little Tesla coils
going on in those eyes.

He looks at me, and smiles. Then he bends down a little,
tousles my hair, and takes my face in his hands. "Am I glad
to see you, Chip."

He turns to Bobo. "Well, well. And who do we have here?"
"His name is Bobo."
Tesla bends down even closer, looking into Bobo's eyes.
"Hmmm. Seems to be a lot going on in there, eh Bobo?"
Bobo reaches up and honks Tesla's nose with his little alien
hand, and we both laugh.

But I'm not here for the warm fuzzies. "Okay.
Introductions, check. Now let's get the hell out of here." I
tie the rope around the three of us. Nice and tight.

And the other end of the rope goes slack.

I pull frantically at it, waiting to feel some tension. Nothing.
Shit. Pull, pull, pull, I'm coiling it at my feet as fast as I can.
I get to the end.

The rope's been cut.

I look up.

It's WHO.

20
Who's Calling

From: Chip Collins
To: Julie Taylor
Date: June 4, 2015 5:43am
Who's calling

Dearest darling Julie,

No, I'm afraid it's not Chip this time. It's WHO. Actually, I do have a name, but it wouldn't make any sense to you.

After I neutralized Chip, during his pathetic attempt at rescuing the equally pathetic Nikola Tesla, I claimed his belongings, including this mobile phone. I've read his emails to you, and let me tell you, it's quite sweet. The boy really is in love with you. But he's a dunce, really.

Well, not completely. Chip was smart enough, along with Tesla, to piece together a fair picture of my plan. And since you'll never read this correspondence anyway, let me share the rest. For fun.

I have learned that possibility is not a given. Possibilities, and the infinite universes they spawn, can be eliminated. I won't go into the details of how – I'm afraid your feeble mind cannot comprehend such things – but let me provide this example: I could, at a whim, eliminate the possibility of you marrying this imbecile Chip. Gone. The possible universe where you marry him and live happily ever after, could be gone in an instant. (You would thank me for that one later, I believe.)

But why am I doing all this, you ask?

It's simple. Once all possibilities are eliminated, once there is only one outcome to all events, the multiverse will be gone, and only one universe will remain – the one whose outcomes I HAVE CHOSEN. I will, in a short time, rule that last single universe with the power of a god. Is it too grand to believe myself a god? Ask the beings in the universes I've already collapsed. (Oh, I'm sorry, you can't. They no longer exist.)

But don't worry, dear Julie, I'll take care of your Chip. You may even meet him one last time. Because, you see, I'm saving your universe for last.

Now, how do you type a lingering, evil laugh on a phone?

Love always,
WHO

Part Three
Saving the Multiverse

21
Bee's Knees

From: Margaret Thatcher
To: Julie Taylor
Date: June 16, 2015 3:27pm
Subject: Chip

Julie,

Pete here. Using Meg's phone. Long story. Chip made me promise to write you emails if anything happened to him. I hate writing.

But something happened.

We sent him into the prison to rescue Nikola Tesla. Now they're both trapped there. I have our copy of the journal, but neither of them is writing back.

I'm sorry, Julie. I think Chip is dead.

- Pete

Dear Julie,

If you get a note from Pete, delete it. I'm fine.

I mean, I'm not fine, but I'm still alive. I'm writing to you on a scrap of paper I found in my pocket because WHO (that GIANT DOUCHE) took my cell phone, and Tesla's journal, and all our shit. So now we have no way to communicate with Pete. And no way out. So yeah, we're all screwed – REALLY screwed, every last one of us including you, if WHO keeps doing what he's doing.

But I'm not dead yet. I've officially decided to start looking at the bright side:
A) I'm not dead. Yet.
B) My friends aren't dead. Yet.
C) I got to meet Nikola Tesla. (Also not dead yet.)
D) He's really cool. I mean, old as the hills, but cool.

And I think it was cool for him to meet me too – I mean, who wouldn't want to meet me, right? – but after the initial tail wagging and high fives, I notice he looks like his best friend died.
"Hey Nikola, you okay? Come on, cheer up. We're gonna get you out of here."
"Chip, meeting you has reminded me. I cannot help but feel that I'm responsible for your dire situation. And not only for you and your friends, but for this danger to the entire multiverse. The INTERDIMENSIONAL TRANSFER APPARATUS and the INTERDIMENSIONAL NAVIGATION CONTROLLER, and who knows what other of my inventions, are being used for evil. This is all because of my inventions."

"So… why'd you invent them?"

"You have an interesting way of trying to cheer me up, Chip."

"Wait. No. That came out wrong. You invented amazing things to be used for *good*, right? That's why you invented them. And just in this one case, some freak dipshit decides to use it for bad. Really bad. *End-of-everything* bad. So we're totally fucked, yeah. Probably as good as dead. But you shouldn't feel bad about it."

"Perhaps we should stop talking for a while."

"No. Listen, it's like a knife. If we didn't have knives, we couldn't hunt for dinner, clear the way through the forest, cut down tree branches for shelter. Basically, we couldn't have even survived. And then suddenly some asshole stabs somebody. Should the guy who invented the knife feel responsible?"

"No. Of course not."

"Well?"

"Hmm. You have a point. I shall ponder that a while. You know, Chip, you are one smart fellow."

"Wow. Nobody ever said that before."

"I can see why."

"Ouch. You have an interesting way of cheering *me* up."

"I'm sorry. No. I meant that there's much more to you than meets the eye. That's a good thing."

"Cool. So, what – like a *chemist* smart, or *engineer* smart, or *political leader* smart, or *philosopher* smart?"

Tesla thinks for a second. "Let's just leave it at smart."

So after a while (days? a year?) it's clear that having me around is getting Tesla back to an optimistic place. WHO's off somewhere being a dick, so whether we like it or not we have time to get to know each other (Bobo's here, but he's doing his perfectly-motionless thing). And here's what I learn about life from him:

If Nikola Tesla was Writing a Self-Help Book, These are the Six Things You Would Learn:

1. Don't Hesitate. If you're ever stuck, wondering whether you should stick your neck out and take that new job, or tell that girl exactly how you feel about her, or try that weird-looking indian food, Tesla would tell you to go for it. Shit, he invented an INTERDIMENSIONAL TRANSFER APPARATUS (all caps, of course) and walked (watch your head on the door) into other dimensions! At eighty-six! Balls.

2. Hesitate. Okay, totally contradicts *Thing You Would Learn #1*, but not the way Tesla tells it. He'd say that before you even get to a moment of decision, you should already know your options (so when the time comes, you don't hesitate - get it?). For example, jump on that new job, but you should already know how you can compensate the lower salary to make rent. Or go to town on that indian food, but you should already have TUMS and Mylanta in your medicine cabinet. And probably a toilet brush.

3. Don't waste time. Tesla never owned a TV, and he definitely didn't have Facebook. (He laughed when I told him about it. "Ha! Hogwash!") He's always just had goals, and marches toward them, no matter what. No distractions. (Not even a girlfriend. Really? Good for him – me, I like me the babes.

Uh, you, I mean, not other babes. Other babes gross me out. You're the only true babe.)

4. Live in a hotel. Okay, I'm kidding with this one, but it's strangely cool, right? He actually lived a simple life in the New Yorker Hotel with his pigeons. Me? I'd live in the Waldorf Astoria. And I'd have a team of butlers and chefs and masseuses and shit. (Hey, if I'm going to fantasize, I'm going all the way. You know what? Add a personal pilot that picks me up from my rooftop helipad to take me to my polo club in the Hamptons. "To the club, Jeeves! And step on it, my good man!")

5. Light the world. Life is too short to screw things up for other people. So use your gifts, take them to the absolute max, and BUILD something that spreads some light. Whatever you can. Even if the most you do is build a relationship with the girl you love. That's lighting the world. Or help that old lady across the street. Or call your dad even if it's the last thing you want to do. Or, in the case of Tesla, invent alternating current, and the radio, radar, x-rays, hydro-electric power, and the ITA. And if you invent the knife so people can eat, and some schmuck uses it to stab somebody, it's not your fault. (I added that last part.)

6. Avoid being abducted by an evil being who's bent on destroying the multiverse.
Self-explanatory.

"Chip, what are you writing?"

"I'm writing to Julie. Telling her all the cool stuff about you."

"*Cool.* I assume that doesn't mean cold."

"No. Cool is good. Awesome. What word did they use for that back in the day?"

"You mean slang? Let's see. Perhaps *berries*. Or nifty. Or jake."

"Okay, cool. I'm writing all the stuff about you that's simply *berries*."

Tesla grins. "You're fairly *jake* yourself, my young adventurer. And this Julie? She sounds like the *cat's pajamas*."

"Cat's pajamas, huh? Yeah. She is. Hey, what's slang for she's beautiful?"

"She's *keen*."

"Smart?"

"She *knows her onions*."

"Wonderful?"

"She's the *bee's knees*."

But before I can catch up on any more old-timey slang to describe you, I hear a sound.

"BEEZNEEZ."

What the hell was that? Huh. Must have been my imagination. This place is starting (starting? ha!) to get to me.

"BEEZNEEZ."

Wait. No. I definitely heard it. Both of us did.

"Chip, I thought you said Bobo doesn't speak."

"He doesn't."

"BEEZNEEZ."

Holy shit.
Bobo's talking!

"Bobo! Buddy! You've been holding out on me!" I skootch over, and put Bobo right between me and Tesla. "So, you little sneak, what else can you say?"

"BEEZNEEZ."

"Come on. You can do better than that. How about Hello?"

"BEEZNEEZ."

"Greetings, earthlings?"

"BEEZNEEZ."

After about fifteen minutes of this, I'm like "Okay, shut the fuck up, Bobo. Bee's knees, I get it. This isn't fun anymore."

"BEEZNEEZ."

Oh God. Somebody please shut Bobo up or I'm going to kill him myself.

From: Margaret Thatcher
To: Julie Taylor
Date: June 16, 2015 3:27pm
Subject: Re: Chip

Julie,

It's Pete again. There's been a development.

Bobo Two is making sounds. Like a french person saying "business." "*Beezneez.*" But that doesn't make any sense.

I'll keep you posted. Not that you're going to see this, but I promised Chip. Wait - why did I promise Chip? He talks me into the stupidist shit. If he lives through this, I'm going to kick his ass.

- Pete

P.S. Meg (the girl who's phone I'm using) is great. I'm thinking long term with her. In other words, I won't be taking her camping with you guys any time soon.

Dear Julie,

I think me and Tesla figured something out. I don't know if it'll help us escape and find Pete and Meg, but it's something.

To review:

• As I (gallantly) attempt to rescue Tesla, WHO cuts the rope. He laughs at me. "You think a simple rope would have worked? Who do you think built this prison, a five-year-old?" I give him the finger. He looks at it blankly.

• Then WHO proceeds to kick my ass (don't worry, I've had much worse from Pete).

• Then WHO takes all our stuff, including Tesla's copy of the journal. (Btw, originally, he only took Tesla's INController. He let Tesla keep the journal. Maybe to see if he would come up with more cool inventions and shit, I don't know. I guess he didn't realize Tesla was using it to communicate with us. According to Tesla, he just looked through it at first, and ripped out a few pages in the middle. Maybe he ran out of toilet paper. Whatever.) Anyway, now he took the whole thing. Dick.

• Then I catch WHO reading my cell phone emails, and he's laughing. LAUGHING! Motherfucker. Those are my personal heartfelt emails to you, and this total dickhead motherfucker is mocking me. Yeah, well you'll get yours, WHO (or Emperor Penisface, or whatever your real name is). Then he leaves. Good. I hate him.

• With nothing to do and no way to communicate with Pete, we just sit around talking over our options and getting to know each other. Good times.

• Then Bobo starts talking.

Well, not talking, but repeating the same (super fucking annoying) phrase over and over. Bee's knees. What is it about those words? Could he have picked a less annoying phrase to say? Like *'Chip, do you mind if I tell you again how awesome you are?'*

"Nikola. Come on. You can figure this out. Can he talk or can't he? And does this even help us?"

"Hmmm. I believe it may help. I've been thinking about the two Bobos. How their special connection may, in fact, be quite useful to our escape. And we will need to communicate with Pete to ensure success. So any spoken words are a good beginning – even if it's only 'Bee's knees'."

"BEEZNEEZ."

"Shhhh! Nikola! God, you want him to start all over again?"
"I was thinking perhaps if I recite a long passage, he'll repeat something I say, and that will give us more clues."
"Okay. But don't make it something annoying."
"Right. A-HEM. *When in the course of human events, it becomes necessary for one people to dissolve...*"

Okay, first of all, how the hell does Tesla know the entire Declaration of Independence by heart? And second, do you have any idea how long it takes to say it out loud? Man, the founding fathers were a bunch of windbags. Anyway, he finally gets done, and... nothing. Bobo's just sitting there, patting his belly and repeating my new favorite phrase.

"BEEZNEEZ. BEEZNEEZ. BEEZNEEZ."

"You know what, Nikola? I don't know why we're wasting our time. This isn't going to help. We're stuck. Fuck."

"STUCKFUCK."

Huh?

"STUCKFUCK."

Bobo's tugging at my shirt sleeve, blabbering away. "Okay, it's official. Bobo is doing this just to piss me off. And it's working."
"Wait a moment. I think you may have unlocked something here."
"Really? The fact that Bobo's brain is broken? Great."
"Patience, Chip. Let me try something. Bobo, *Take Lake.*"

"TAKELAKE. TAKELAKE. TAKELAKE."

"Bravo, Chip! That's it!"
"What?"
"Rhymes! Bobo can speak in rhyme!"
"Wonderful. Bobo's a poet, and he didn't even know it. So?"
"So my idea becomes more plausible: if we can use Bobo and his identical counterpart as a conduit to communicate with Pete and Meg, the odds of our escape increase dramatically."
"Hold on. If Bobo can talk in rhyme, how come he can't even say his own name?"

The Three Rules of Bobo Speak

After an hour of testing on Bobo (trust me, I got him to say as many curses as possible, I was surprised how many words rhyme with fuck), it turns out there are specific strange conditions to getting Bobo to say something:

1. It has to be *different* words that rhyme. So "Take Lake" is okay, but "Bo Bo" isn't. Poor guy can't even say his own name (which I made up, so it's not really his name, so he probably doesn't give a rat's ass).

2. It has to be two words together without any words between. So "fuck a duck" won't work. It has to be "fuck duck." Three words like "Fuck duck schmuck" will work too. Nice touch.

3. Each word has to be one syllable. So we can't use "Petesaveusrightnow Shmeetesaveusrightnow." Damn.

And I know you're thinking this is bat-shit crazy, but Tesla explains that there's actually a real condition called *Spasmodic Dysphonia* (he wouldn't shit me, right?) that limits a person's speech to rhymes, or a foreign accent, or individual words, or no speech at all. So Bobo's exposure to the ITA might have caused a similar condition. I know, super-interesting, right? You know what? When I get home I'll write a research paper called *"Spasmodic Dysphonia in Unidentified Interdimensional Creatures,"* and we can both read it while we drink too many vodka and tonics and rub each other's feet, and laugh our asses off at how ridiculous this whole thing was. Actually, scratch the first part about writing the paper – let's go directly to feet rubbing and vodka and tonic drinking and laughing our asses off. Put it on your calendar.

Anyway, after lots of trial and error, me and Tesla come up with a message for Pete, and keep our fingers crossed that this *Bobo-One-as-a-Conduit-to-Bobo-Two* thing works.

Pete's going to be so proud!

From: Margaret Thatcher
To: Julie Taylor
Date: June 16, 2015 3:27pm
Subject: Re: Chip

Julie,

Pete here. Your boyfriend is a fucking idiot.

He's got nothing better to do than use Bobo to send me nonsense messages, mostly using words that rhyme with "fuck."

- Pete

From: Margaret Thatcher
To: Julie Taylor
Date: June 16, 2015 3:27pm
Subject: Re: Chip

Julie,

Pete here. Disregard that last email. Meg figured out that
the Bobo messages needed decoding. My bad.

And because I know you have the same sense of humor as
Chip, I figured you would enjoy the last message he sent
through Bobo:

*"YOMOFO WEBE LIVEDIVE STOPDROP WEBE GUNFUN
YOOZTOOZ BOLO BOWZLOWZ AZPAZ CONRON DURU
ITSHIT FORBOR SCAPEGRAPE STOPDROP STANDBAND
BYDY STRUKSFUCKS STOPDROP CONRON FERMPERM
WITHPITH NEWBREW MESSTRESS AGEPAGE
STOPDROP PEEWEE ESSPRESS TELLPRELL JOOLDROOL
STOPDROP SHILLQUILL LUVDUV THISMISS
OUTSPOUT."*

Literal translation:
"YO MO FO WE LIVE (STOP) WE GUN YOOZ BO BOWZ
AS CON DU IT FOR SCAPE (STOP) STAND BY STRUKS
(STOP) CON FERM WITH NEW MESS AGE (STOP) PEE
ESS TELL JOOL (STOP) SHILL LUV THIS (OUT)"

Actual Translation:
Yo motherfucker – we're alive! We're going to use the two Bobos as conduits for our escape. Stand by for instructions. Confirm with a new message.
P.S. Tell Julie. She'll love this.

Later,
- Pete

P.S. Listen, I do need to tell you this: I know I call Chip an idiot, but he's changed. I've seen things from him – courage, smarts, sacrifice – that I just didn't think he had in him. You might want to think about giving him a second chance. Just saying.

P.P.S. Don't get me wrong. He's still an idiot 90% of the time.

22
The Great(ish) Escape

Dear Julie,

Okay, so we go back and forth with Pete (it was hilarious the first couple of times, but I'm pretty done with the *talking-through-Bobo* thing), and establish that we can communicate, and help each other with the next critical step Tesla has planned.

And since Tesla thinks too fast for me to write all his craziness down, I'm making him tell you himself.

Dear Ms. Taylor,

First, let me introduce myself: I am **Nikola Tesla**, the inventor of the **INTERDIMENSIONAL TRANSFER APPARATUS**. If you ever receive Chip's correspondence, please note that this term should be spelled in ALL CAPITAL LETTERS at all times. He may also refer to it as the "ITA," which I find acceptable.

Second, I must say that it is a pleasure to "meet" you, as it were. Your beau Chip has told me much about you, and we've agreed that you are, in fact, the cat's pajamas – a slang term from my day. As a side note, Chip has taught me slang from his era as well, although most of it I would never repeat to a fair lady such as yourself, for fear of being smacked directly in the face.

Third, I have heard that Chip may not have treated you as well as deserved recently. But I would vouch that the Chip I have come to know is honest, courageous, clever, and contrite: I hope you can grant him forgiveness. (Although it is true that he can be almost too much to bear when he endlessly prattles on about this or that! And he feels he must include several swear words in every single sentence! Tsk!)

Finally, at Chip's request, I will outline our escape plan:

Step 1: Expose the electrical circuitry of the ITA

As Chip may have described to you in previous correspondence, I designed the INTERDIMENSIONAL TRANSFER APPARATUS with electrical outlets, to power the INTERDIMENSIONAL NAVIGATION CONTROLLER, under every third doorway, eighteen feet apart. By fashioning a screwdriver from my index fingernail (I have been growing it for quite some time for such a purpose), we will unscrew the plate, remove the outlet, and expose the bare wiring. Pete will do the same on their side, albeit without a fingernail, but a screwdriver from among Meg's tools. On another side note, I am quite excited to meet Meg. She seems to have a "kick-ass" intellect, as Chip would say. (Sorry. I simply had to indulge in one of Chip's colorful phrases!)

Step 2: Send a massive electrical charge through Bobo

At precisely the same moment, Pete and I will plunge the exposed, live wires into Bobo's flesh. (Poor Bobo. Chip has assured me that they have previously electrocuted Bobo, and that he has survived, or even thrived on, the experience. I hope he is right. I have never killed a living thing before.)

Of course, I have tried using electricity many times to break the continuity of the prison's containment field. But short circuits and such, acting strictly within the prison, have failed.

Now, at least theoretically, two simultaneous electrocutions, from <u>inside and outside</u> the prison – the first passing from Bobo One towards Bobo Two, the second passing from Bobo Two towards Bobo One – should collide in the middle and generate a massive power surge and overload. This in turn should create a breach in the prison's containment field, allowing us to...

<u>Step 3: Pass through to safety</u>
Once together on the other side, and with the aide of the second INTERDIMENSIONAL NAVIGATION CONTROLLER, we will navigate to a dimension that can help us in our quest to stop WHO. However, one step at a time.

I will now hand the floor, as it were, back to Chip.

Yours Very Truly,
Nikola Tesla
January 7, 1943

Dear Julie,

So we're ready. WHO is off collapsing another universe (which, I think I've mentioned, hurts like a motherfucker, btw), so we're pretty confident he'll be gone for a while.

We get everything ready: expose the wires, coordinate with Pete, get Bobo into position. We're all sitting on the floor of the hallway, ready to jump into this breach thing Tesla's talking about.

"Pardon me, Chip."
"Yeah?"
"Are you certain about doing this to Bobo?"
"Of course. Here, look, he'll tell you himself. Hey Bobo, tell Nikola what you think of us electrocuting you with these wires."

Bobo gives Nikola the finger.
"BEEZNEEZ."

"See? We're all set."
"All right. But there is one other small thing."
"Uh-oh."
"There is a slight possibility that this dual electrocution will cause a chain reaction effect, much like what happens on an atomic scale in a nuclear fission reaction."
"Okay, english?"
"We could do worse than WHO, with a cascading collapse of universes that doesn't end. Which would hasten that which we are trying to prevent in the first place. The end of everything."

Ugh. Again with the *end-of-everything* talk. God I hate that shit. So of course you pop into my head. And I think back to the last time I saw you. And before you start deleting this email – if I promise this is the only time I rehash what happened in April, just to get it out there on the table in case this is my last chance, is that okay? I promise. Bear with me.

It was a rainy night, like a boring middle-of-the-week Tuesday. You came over after work, in this shitstorm mood about how Lisa at work was a total bitch to you. No smile, no hug, just a big cloud of negative. And you ranted on for like a half an hour. And this wasn't the first time.

So I just freaked out. Like, I had enough of my own bullshit to deal with – how could I possibly have enough of whatever it takes to help you deal with yours, too? Wasn't love just about having fun? And *forgetting* all the bullshit of normal life when you're together?

So I ran away. In my own demented way, I thought one person's bullshit was better than two people's bullshit.

I was wrong.

Here's what I found out the second I stepped into the ITA: that when you find yourself in that moment where life is nothing *but* bullshit, when you don't know which way is out, when you're trapped and scared and alone, you would give anything to be with that person, no matter how much extra baggage they came with. And that's when I had the flash of truth:

Love is not just the fun and the good times –
it's the bearing of each other's bullshit,
the wanting to bear that great weight together,
the lifting each other up. That's love.

I know I sound like a broken record at this point. I know
if Pete was reading this he'd be rolling his eyes and
pretending to gag himself. But I don't care. I need you to
know again. One more time. To know that this is keeping
me going. I have walked this hallway for a year, for a
decade, forever, for one reason: to come home, and pick up
your backpack full of bullshit, and help you carry it, while
you reach over and help me carry mine. And I can't wait for
the moment we realize that with both of us carrying, it's not
so heavy after all.

"Chip? Did you hear me? Chip?"
"Huh? Oh, yeah, Nikola, end of everything. Cool. How
slight of a possibility?"
"One in a hundred, perhaps."

I grab the wires from Tesla.
"Fuck the one percent. Let's go home."
And I jam them into Bobo's chest.

Holy shit.

I hope this isn't the end of everything.
But it sure looks like it.

Dear Julie,

KA-BLAAAAMMMMM!!!

No.

SKACHOWWWWWWW!!!

No.

SCRUMPHPAAHHSHGHGH!!!

No. Whatever. It's no use. There's no word for what we're feeling/seeing/hearing. Except it's REALLY bright, and REALLY loud, and REALLY FUCKING SCARY.

I jump into Nikola's arms, screaming.
"Nikola! It's the end!"
Over the deafening sound, I can barely hear him yelling back. "No, Chip! It's not the end! It's the beginning! Look!"
He points through an opening, at the center of the brightest light I've ever seen, and I can barely make it out, it looks a million miles away, but it's there...

Pete!

I let go of Tesla, and push him towards the breach. He picks up Bobo (who's hopefully only momentarily dead) and dives in. I'm right behind him. I dive.

But I stop. What the fuck?

I look back.

WHO's holding my damn foot.

Dear Julie,

You know how the bad guys are always really ugly, like hardly human at all, with cancerous growths all over them, long brown fingernails, face tattoos, missing teeth and shit? Not this WHO guy. I REAALLLYY hate to say this, but...

WHO is cuddly.

I swear to God, that's the first word that pops into my head when I get a good look at him. Cuddly.

So he's holding onto my foot as I try to escape, and I'm kicking his head with my other foot, while Pete and Meg are trying to pull me out of the breach by my hands. Then one of my kicks knocks off WHO's hood, and I'm like:

"Holy shit. *Santa?*"

Seriously. Santa Claus. Or Gandalf the White. Or Hagrid from Harry Potter. Dumbledore. Or some other old, kind, benevolent guy with a long, white, flowing beard who watches out for you. Even his eyes are warm and friendly. He smiles. I get the urge to sit on his lap and tell him what I want for Christmas. And it's crazy fucking loud, but I can here him whisper...

"Chip. Come back. You forgot your mobile phone."

I'm slipping. Pete and Meg and now Tesla are trying like hell to pull me to safety, but I'll admit it – I'm thinking *maybe this guy WHO isn't so bad after all. Look at him, for crying out loud! And he wants me to have my cell phone back.*

That's kind of sweet. So I let go of one hand and reach back for it. Pete and Meg are screaming, but I can't hardly hear them over the roar of the breach. I can only hear WHO's whisper. He extends my phone a little closer.

"That's it, Chip. Just a little more. You're almost home."

Wait.

Home.

Where is home? Is home with this cuddly old man who might bring me presents if I'm a good kid? I'll probably get hot chocolate too. Whenever I want. I wonder if he has elves.
And then I remember.
Fuck no.
Santa's not real *(sorry for the spoiler, kids)*.
Home is with you.

I reach back toward WHO even further, smiling at him, stretching my hand out, and he meets me halfway with the phone in his hand. I snatch it from his fingers and look right in his eyes. "Thanks for the phone, bitch." Then I kick him in the temple with my free foot. "And that's for laughing at my emails, you dick. Pete! Let's go!"

I swing my hand back to Pete and with one last giant heave, they all get me through the breach. *Whew!*

Wait. Except my foot. WHO's still got a pit-bull hold on my foot, no matter how much we kick and pull.

WHO smiles, and whispers again. "All right then, Chip. It looks like I'll just have to join you and Tesla and your friends. It'll be fun." And he begins crawling up my leg, through to our side of the breach.

"GET HIM THE FUCK OFF! CLOSE THE BREACH NIKOLA!! CLOSE THE BREACH!!"

What I didn't know at the time, though, was that Tesla had no idea how to close the breach once it was open. It was an uncontrolled phenomenon that might last for one second, or one year, or forever. And as he's trying to explain this, yelling over the sound, and we're all pulling and kicking like mad, and I'm prying WHO off me, and even Bobo is biting WHO's fingers, and it looks like all is lost…

SCHLUNK.

The breach closes. Silence.

Whew again! Finally. We're free!

I look up at Pete and Meg and Tesla standing over me, and I smile. But they're not smiling back. They're looking past me.

"What?"

I look down. What a mess. There's blood everywhere.

Oh God. I'm going to throw up.

23
Hey!
I liked that foot!

From: Chip Collins
To: Julie Taylor
Date: June 4, 2015 5:43am
Hey! I liked that foot!

Hi Julie,

Good news/bad news.

Good news is I got my cell phone back, so I can email you instead of scratching notes on bits of paper and sending them to you inside bottles like Robinson Crusoe.

The bad news? My fucking foot is gone. My right foot. My second favorite foot. Gone. How the fuck am I going to drive?

And yeah, I'm crying. But this time Pete doesn't think I'm a baby. He saw the breach close right on my ankle and WHO's hand. The blood everywhere. Pieces of fingers, and blood, and my fucking stump of a leg. Gross. Pete takes my hand. "Dude, hold on. We've got you."

In appreciation, I throw up on him.

By the time I pass out, and then come to and throw up on Pete again, and start crying again, the whole team is already down to business.

"I'll tie a turniquet from the rope."
"Nikola, keep pressure on it."
"Is there a rag somewhere? I have Chip puke all over me."

Meanwhile, the Bobos are just standing there. They're back from being electrocuted, good as new I guess, but just staring at this whole scene, the blood and the frantic activity, and of course me puking. Suddenly they walk right into the middle of us.

"STOPDROP."

Pete's not amused. "Bobos, get the fuck out of the way!"

"STOPDROP."

"Not the time! Back off!"
And then Meg does the lightbulb thing (she's always doing it. You can tell when she gets an idea, because she raises one of her eyebrows and taps her chin and kind of smiles. It's sort of cute – except when you're covered in your own blood and vomit). "Wait, Pete. One second."
And one second is all the Bobos need. They immediately kneel down by my ankle. I manage a whisper. "Hey, maybe they have some kind of healing power. They're messiahs, you know."
But instead of healing me, in perfect unison, the Bobos start chewing their own hands off.

"OHMYGODWHATTHEFUCK?!?! THAT'S DISGUSTING!!! ISN'T ONE MISSING LIMB ENOUGH?!?!"

And now I know a new answer to that joke:

What's grosser than gross?
Two furry aliens chewing off their own hands
over a big puddle of blood and puke and finger pieces,
and some poor guy who's foot just got chopped off
by a breach collapse.

Oh, and that's also when I pass out again.

From: Chip Collins
To: Julie Taylor
Date: June 4, 2015 5:43am
Re: Hey! I liked that foot!

Hi Julie,

Okay, so I wasn't awake for any of this, but apparently some pretty crazy shit happened while I was out. I'm still weak, so I made Tesla type it out for you:

> At first, we were all astonished at what was taking place. The identical Bobos were kneeling over poor Chip's lower legs, gnawing their own flesh. With so much gore, I dare say I nearly discharged the contents of my own stomach!

> Before Pete, Meg or I could remove the two clearly disturbed creatures, the Bobos regurgitated their newly chewed flesh onto Chip's ankle, quickly molding it with their remaining hands around the bloody stump where his foot had been.

> We stood in shock as the next events unfolded: the flesh began to adhere itself to Chip's own – and grow! Within the space of ten minutes, both Bobos' hands had grown back, and Chip had grown a new foot! All limbs as good as new!

> With one notable exception.

From: Chip Collins
To: Julie Taylor
Date: June 4, 2015 5:43am
Re: Hey! I liked that foot!

Hi Julie,

"A FURRY FOOT?!?"

"A FURRY FUCKING FOOT?!?!"

Sure, Tesla tries explaining how magical this all is, but I'm
not buying. Who wants a furry fucking foot?

"Chop it off again. I'd rather have no foot."
"Dude, you're in shock. Calm down."
"And how the fuck did I get a furry foot?! The last I looked,
I didn't even have a foot! Can somebody tell me what the
fuck is going on? And another thing…"
And Meg slaps me.
"I'm sorry. But this is a good thing. Let me explain."
And because I don't want to get slapped again, I cower and
listen to Meg's way-too-techy explanation.

**Meg's Way-Too-Techy Explanation
of What Happened to My Foot:**
We already knew from Meg's previous way-too-
techy explanation about Bobo that he can regenerate
himself like a starfish, using asexual reproduction.

But that's not all. Because starfish have cells like stem cells that are immature, they can grow into any limb or body part needed (whatever, she could be making all this shit up and I'd have to believe it because I'm ignorant). So Bobo's chewed flesh (gross) somehow bonded with my own, triggering a signal to grow back my foot. However, because it was a mixture of Bobo's and my own DNA, I now have a stupid-looking furry foot.

"I don't care. I'd still rather have no foot. Nikola, you're a man of reason. Would you want a furry alien foot? Truly, deep down in your heart? Wouldn't you rather have a nice pair of crutches? Or a hand-carved mahogany peg leg? Please cut this thing off, will you?"

"Chip. We are obviously not going to cut off your new foot. Can you not see even one positive thing in this?"

Hmm. I hesitate. I look down at it. "Well, it'll never get cold."

"Excellent. Anything else?"

"I'll always win bar bets."

"Um, all right, fair enough. Now anything more obvious?"

"I can walk, I guess."

"*Exactly!* And with shoes and socks on, others won't even notice."

Pete joins the feel-good party. "And dude – I'm sure it'll look normal if you shave it."

"Nice. Fuck you."

"Hey, and you can hump your *own* leg now!"

"Now really fuck you. That was low."

"Sorry, dude. Got carried away. Here, let me help you up."

So him and Tesla grab me and get me on my feet, and wouldn't you know – I feel fine. Like totally normal. So I kick Pete in the nuts with my new foot. "How's that for a leg hump?" (Don't worry, Julie. Pete's got balls of steel, and shrugged it off like it was a gentle breeze.)

Then I go over to the Bobos and bend down and pat them both on the head. This sucks for sure, but I guess a furry foot is better than no foot. "Thanks, dudes."

"BEEZNEEZ."

24
We Should
Really Get Going

From: Chip Collins
To: Julie Taylor
Date: June 4, 2015 5:43am
We should really get going

Hi Julie,

So we're standing there, it's been probably ten minutes, discussing alien feet and our near miss with the breach, and Meg is falling all over her new crush Tesla, her idol, and it's awesome because Pete is getting jealous. Jealous of eighty-six year old Nikola Tesla. Like red-face jealous. I love it.

She's even stumbling over herself. "..and, and, and I am in awe of your work with electromagnetic induction. Believe it or not, *believe it or not*, only now are some commercial enterprises beginning to leverage your concepts for wireless energy transmission. Simply wow. Wow. You are still so far ahead of our times."
Tesla allows himself a sheepish grin. "I am flattered, Miss Thatcher. Speaking of that work, I think I've solved some of the coherence and range limitation problems. Would you like me to share what I've devised?"

Meg's knees go weak, and those freaking eyelashes start fluttering like crazy. Pete actually steps directly between them, like Tesla's some goon hitting on his girl at a bar. "Um. This is nice. But shouldn't we be talking about stopping WHO?"

"WHO!!!"

300 | Rob Dircks

"Chip dude, calm down. I'm talking to Nikola."

"NO! WHO!! LOOK!!!"

They all turn to the direction I'm pointing, down the hall. And sure enough, way down, just close enough on the horizon to see, is WHO. And he's charging this way. Pretty damn fast, too.

But instead of running away, I freeze. And then I remember and smile. *Santa's back!* Man, I never knew Santa could run like that. He's probably rushing over here to make sure I get that Xbox I wanted for Christmas.

But Pete ruins my Christmas fantasy and grabs me.

"RUN!!!"

Woah. Pete snaps me back to reality. (Mental note: gotta watch out for that crazy whammy shit WHO can pull. It's like he can hypnotize you. Btw, thanks again Pete, for saving my ass for the umpteen millionth time. If you ever get tired of doing that I'm a dead man.) So anyway, we start running like hell, trying to stay ahead of WHO, without a plan. Just run forever, I guess that's the plan. Good plan.

"TURN LEFT HERE!"
"WHY?!"
"NO IDEA!"
"OKAY! GOOD!"
"TURN RIGHT!"
"SHOULD I ASK?"
"NO!"

So it goes on like that for a while, all of us screaming like baboons at each other and tearing down the hallway, banging into turns and doors and shit. And I can see Tesla running out of steam (doing a damn good job for eighty-six, but still), and Pete's carrying *both* Bobos, so he's not going to last much longer either, and fucking WHO is like an olympic marathon sprinter or something, no signs of giving up. Even with one fingerless, bleeding hand. If we don't come up with something quick, we're fucked.

"WE HAVE TO DUCK INTO A DOOR!"
"NO! HE'LL JUST FOLLOW US IN!"
"OKAY! NIKOLA! IT'S ABOUT TIME FOR SOME OF THAT GENIUS!!"

Just then, Nikola trips. And he skids on his ass like ten yards down the hallway. (I would laugh, it's totally funny, it would get like a billion hits on YouTube, but you know, it's Nikola Tesla, and also we're all about to be taken back into WHO's psychedelic prison.) He's laying there, looking pretty pathetic. (I know, I know, me at eighty six will look ten times more pathetic.)

"Chip! Continue without me. I'll try to…"
"…to what? Fight WHO? No. Duh. You're coming. Let's go."

I quick bend down and pick up Tesla. I put one arm around my shoulder, and Meg puts his other arm over her. And as the three of us and Pete turn around to run again, we stop.

"Here. Hurry. This way."

What the fuck?

From: Chip Collins
To: Julie Taylor
Date: June 4, 2015 5:43am
Re: We really should get going

Hi Julie,

You're not going to believe this.

(Wait – I should just stop saying that, right? Like everything that's happened since I started writing you these emails nobody would believe anyway. *Shit's crazy. Don't ask.*)

Anyway, standing there right in front of us is this guy in a fancy futuristic biker suit, shiny black and silver, with a motorcycle helmet and gloves and everything. He reaches his hand out to us and talks. His helmet's closed, though, so we can barely hear him.

"Hhrrmphtthhwy."
"Uh, what?"
"Hhrrmphtthhwy."
"It's a little hard to hear. With the helmet. Muffled, you know? It's like 'Hhrrmphtthhwy'."
So the guy bends down, takes his helmet off, and lifts his head to look at us. "I said 'Hurry, this way.' Is that better?"

And Meg faints.

It's Pete.

From: Chip Collins
To: Julie Taylor
Date: June 4, 2015 5:43am
Re: We should really get going

Hi Julie,

Holy shit. It's Pete.

Well, another alternate Pete. Like Alternate Badass Biker Pete. "Come on. The door's right over here. Let's go. Bad guy's catching up."

I can't resist. "Dude. Cool biker suit."

Alternate Pete gives me this look like I'm an idiot *(oh yes, it's definitely Pete!)*. "Cool furry foot."

But before I can say "fuck you" to our new friend, Alternate Badass Biker Pete is rushing over to help regular Pete pick up Meg. They stop just long enough to have that weird moment where you smile when you meet your alternate from another dimension.
"Hey bro."
"Hey bro. Listen, we really should get going."
And sure enough, WHO has enlarged from a speck on the horizon to a pretty big-sized bad guy barreling toward us. I can see his bloody stump of a hand. We've got another thirty seconds tops.

So Alternate Badass Biker Pete gets us over to a door, and dials in the combination. I peek over his shoulder. 1-2-3-4. *Of course!*

Chip's Official Moment of Enlightenment About the Door Combinations

Okay, so now it's crystal clear. Our dimension has a combination of 0-0-0-0. Other dimensions have some crazy combination between integers that make it virtually impossible to guess (in addition to the various realities where Tesla, Chip, Pete, or the journals don't exist, so there's no clues that the door even exists). But there must be those dimensions who have easy-to-guess combinations, like 1-2-3-4, and where Tesla's journal was found. Apparently this guy has both. It's official. I'm smart.

"Okay, folks - IN!"

So we all scramble through the doorway. (Meg's turn to hit her head. We're in a rush, but I still have time to laugh. And she still has time to give me the finger.) We cram into this little chamber. It's not another elevator, it's a little bigger, more like a dorm room or something. There are posters of space and stars on the wall, and this big kick-ass-looking gaming system under one of the posters.

"Wait. Won't WHO just follow us right in?"
But Alternate Badass Biker Pete is way ahead of us I guess. "Let him try."

He sits down at the gaming system and hits a button.
The door behind us makes some whooshing and locking
sounds. And then we jolt forward.

"Hold on, people."

Holy shit.
This isn't a dorm room.
That's not a gaming system.
Those aren't posters of stars.
And Alternate Pete's not wearing a badass biker suit.

We're in outer space.

This is some kind of shuttle. The posters are actual
windows. We're out in the middle of fucking space.
Alternate Pete is at the cockpit controls in a space suit
(*question for later: why can't NASA come up with wicked cool
space suits like this?*) and we're hurtling through the void.

"Holy fuck. Wait. Where's the hotel room?"
"Have a look."

Alternate Pete slows down and maneuvers the shuttle
around so we can see where we just came from.

"It's just space. Nothing."
"Give it a second. WHO should be trying to get in right…
about… now…"

And I see it: a little sliver of light, the shape of a doorway. Then a little body comes rushing out, into the vacuum of space, and holds on to the door for dear life. Then the little body claws its way back inside (with only one good hand – I'm impressed) and the doorway closes.

Alternate Pete smiles. Then he says maybe the coolest thing I've ever heard: "Asshole might be able to collapse universes, but he still can't breathe in space."

We all let out a little sigh of relief.

The Bobos, in appreciation I guess, go over and try to hump Alternate Pete's leg. But he shakes them off. "Dudes! Come on, I'm driving."

Meg's adjusting to the gravity in the shuttle, and leans on Pete for support. She squeezes his arm, and manages a smile. "You know, this guy's kind of cute."
"He's me. Of course he's cute. Don't get any ideas."
"Please. But I do have a *million* questions for him." She turns to Alternate Pete. "While we're underway, may I ask you a million questions?"

"Sure. Let me just set our course for Earth Fragment Five."

25
Earth Fragment
Five

From: Chip Collins
To: Julie Taylor
Date: June 4, 2015 5:43am
Earth Fragment Five

Hi Julie,

Earth Fragment Five? Meg's head practically explodes. Now she has *two* million questions, *and* she's having a nerdgasm.

And God, her Q&A session with Alternate Pete would scramble your brains. So instead, while we're being transported to some base in the middle of nowhere, I've decided to condense the entire true story as Alternate Pete relates it into my first easy-to-read mini novel:

Earth Fragment Five:
A Space Odyssey (Based on a True Story)
A Cell Phone Novel by Chip Collins

In the beginning, there was a parallel dimension (I'm assuming you've got the whole infinite parallel dimensions thing down) that was identical to our own, except for one little tiny, itty-bitty difference:

The Alpen-Norton meteor's orbit was off by .000031 degrees.

Now that doesn't sound like a lot, and it wouldn't matter, except that over millions of years this orbit kept getting a wee bit closer to Earth. And in 1904 the meteor buzzed so close that every single person on the planet shit their pants at the same moment. Kersplatt!! (Imagine the dry cleaning bill.)

Unsurprisingly, everybody freaked out – riots, looting, religious extremism, violence, mass suicides. Ah, the good old days.

But finally the hero of our story said "Uh, are we just going to rape and pillage like fucking pirates until we kill each other off, or figure this shit out?" And they all looked at him, and said "Shut the fuck up asshole," bum-rushed him, and hung him up by his thumbs in the town square. (I made that part up - but it's good drama for the novel, right?)

Okay, truth is, they don't kill the guy – they actually listen to him. You know why? Because our story's hero is *Theodore "Rough Rider" Roosevelt*, that's why. President of the United States. The Man on Horseback. The Hero of San Juan Hill. T.R. (Alternate Pete goes on for like five minutes with the nicknames, I had to cough really loud to get him to stop.) Anyway, Roosevelt gathers the world's top astronomers (not astrologers – those motherfuckers were adding to the chaos. He had them all thrown in prison) and they determine that exactly eighty years later, in 1984, the meteor would strike Earth with a direct hit. 100% certainty. Boom.

The End.

Right?

Wrong. Teddy was like "Fuck that shit. I'll be goddamned if my great-grandkids aren't going to have green grass to roll around in, and wild horses to tame, and little red one-room schoolhouses, and all the other shit people do in the early 1900s." *(Actual quote.)*

So from that moment, the Great Earth Trust was born. And the best scientific minds of the time were gathered to form The Great Earth Trust Solution. (And ironically, because everyone on the planet now had a common goal, and no reason to develop atomic bombs and shit, there was relative peace on Earth for the next eighty years. A little accidental benefit of having a giant meteor target your ass!) So who was on this dream team?

• Albert Einstein – "The Quarterback." Known for his imagination as well as insane intellect, his role was to come up with the core idea: how to save as much of humanity as possible, to live beyond the destruction of Earth. Brainstorm new ideas, throw out shitty ones, and be cool. Which he was.

• Marie Curie – "The Elementalist." In charge of finding new base chemicals and materials for construction, shielding, medicines, life support systems, you name it. She rocked it.

• Carl Jung – "The Dreamer." His role was to shape the mindset and psychological adjustments necessary for an entire species to live in radically new circumstances.

• Wilbur and Orville Wright – "The Architects."(In case it's not obvious, I'm making the nicknames up.) Famous for their first airplane flight just a year prior, the brothers would design and begin construction on the massive self-contained living areas across the globe called "iPods."

(Wait – *iPods?* WTF? I interrupt my novel to remind
Alternate Pete that iPods are the little music
players that have been around since 2001. Alternate
Pete reminds me that I don't know what the hell
I'm talking about, and those are called iDrives.
"IHPods" stands for Intraplanetary Habitation
Pods. Spelled I-*H*-Pods. The "h" is silent. Duh.
Of course, Chip! Get with the program!)

And the last member of the Great Earth Trust Solution
Dream Team? The man responsible for an insane new fuel
that powers this whole getup? Drum roll please...

• Nikola Tesla!
  (*Official novel break:* Tesla gasps when he hears his
  name. "One moment, if I may, master Pete. The
  ANTIMATTER COLLECTOR AND AMPLIFIER?
  Could it possibly be real?"
  Alternate Pete grins. "You bet. Mr. Tesla, sir. Your
  invention saved our world."
  "But... the resources required to construct..."
  "Mr. Tesla. It's real. Sadly, the Nikola Tesla from
  our dimension made it only as far as the ITA portal
  in 1943. He died right at the doorway. But *The
  Journal* was intact. Sir, you'll get to see your work
  realized. And there are a LOT of people who'd like
  to say thank you.")

Okay, back to *Earth Fragment Five: A Space Odyssey...*

So Nikola Tesla was on the team, too. And he took FORTY
YEARS to develop the most unbelievable, ass-kicking fuel
collection/amplification/distribution system ever.

See, they knew that they needed a fuel alternative – as traditional petroleum reserves couldn't be counted on when the planet broke into a million pieces. Each of the fifty IHPods (not the music player) would need a massive, efficient fuel source to power artificial breathable atmospheres, infrastructure, farming, industry, communication, blah, blah, blah, supporting the millions of people living in each one, floating around on their little patches of dirt.

But what the hell could they use to power it? Atomic energy as a fuel didn't even exist yet, and Marie Curie already knew that radiation from using radioactive isotopes might be a huge problem. So they were all sitting around banging their heads against the conference room table (except Einstein – he was out getting his hair teased) and Tesla stormed in, waving his journal over his head.

"Antimatter!"

Everyone was like "Dude - you were supposed to bring sandwiches. And what the hell is antimatter?"
"I will return with sandwiches, I apologize. And when I do, I will have the solution to our fuel problem!"

40 YEARS LATER…

So Tesla got kicked out of the Dream Team for talking crazy shit about antimatter (and maybe for not ever returning with sandwiches), but on his deathbed four decades later, he revealed the solution to their fuel problem: The ANTIMATTER COLLECTOR AND AMPLIFIER. (Yes, in all caps.) Then he croaked.

(*Official novel break:* Tesla seems genuinely sad to hear that his counterpart in this dimension died in 1943. Which raises a question: with *infinite* alternative dimensions, aren't versions of us dying all the time? Whatever. I'll just let you ponder that downer thought for a while.)

Anyway, this device (it's huge, and has to be blasted into space to work) collects antimatter from a belt of the stuff about 500 kilometers above Earth, and amplifies its effects. So a single gram of antimatter can power an entire IHPod for three years. Imagine smoking that shit?

So anyway they ditched their less-than-earth-shattering plan (no pun intended), posthumously let Tesla back into the gang, celebrated with (you guessed it) sandwiches, and got to work.

40 MORE YEARS LATER...

October 12, 1984. Impact. Holy hell.

The Earth shattered into twelve main fragments and about a hundred smaller chunks. Thirty-five of the IHPods remained (they had estimated fewer, so this was actually a good number). Lots of people died. But a LOT of people lived.

And they all lived happily ever after.

The End.

From: Chip Collins
To: Julie Taylor
Date: June 4, 2015 5:43am
Re: Earth Fragment Five

Meg's reading over my shoulder. "Woah! Woah. Chip, you can't end it like that! What about us? How do we fit in? What about the journal? And the ITA? And WHO?"
"That'll be in *Earth Fragment Five: A Space Odyssey Book Two.* Come on. Give my fingers a freaking break. One novel at a time."
Alternate Pete laughs. "All your questions will be answered when we get inside, Meg. Look. We're here."

Wow. We've all been so distracted by Alternate Pete's story, we didn't notice our approach. Earth Fragment Five is actually beautiful. Like a little craggy moon, but covered in green and blue. Well, half of it is, I guess the top half. The bottom half is all machines and plumbing and shit. The whole thing seems to me about as big as Maryland. I don't know. I sucked at geography in high school.

Anyway, we start descending through these big, puffy clouds, and I'm like "shouldn't there be a dome or something?"

Alternate Pete laughs again. "It's a little more complicated than that. Even I don't know how it works. You'll have to ask Commander Collins about it."

"Wait. Did you say *Collins*?"

Alternate Pete puts on a shit-eating grin. "Yup. Didn't want to spoil the surprise. Commander Clarence Collins."
Regular Pete sees me turn white as a sheet. "Dude. You okay?"

"Pete, dude. Clarence is my first name."

From: Chip Collins
To: Julie Taylor
Date: June 4, 2015 5:43am
Re: Earth Fragment Five

Hi Julie,

Yeah, holy shit, right?

Clarence "Chip" Collins. That's me.

Heck, I'm pretty sure I never even told YOU my real first
name. It's always just been Chip. When my grandfather
saw me for the first time, he said I looked just like my dad.
A chip off the old block. So Chip it was.

I swear until I went to school I didn't even know. On the
first day of kindergarten Mrs. Ostenfrier is calling out
"Clarence Collins?" and I'm like "cool, there's another kid
with my last name in class!" And she keeps looking around,
and skips over my name until I'm the last one not called.
"And who are you, young man?"
"Chip Collins."
"Not Clarence?"
"Nope."
But I'm kind of getting it at this point, and I start to cry, and
the other kids start laughing. Fucking kids. You won't be
laughing when a firecracker goes off in your underpants,
Danny Boyle.

Woah. Wait, where was I?

Right. Earth Fragment Five.

We're about to meet Commander Clarence Collins. How fucking cool is that? *Commander!* And Alternate Pete over here *reports to him?* I knew somewhere in the infinite possibilities Pete had to report to Chip! I'm stoked.

So anyway, they walk us out of the transport hangar, right to a big black bus. There's a crowd behind some barricades off about fifty feet, somehow these people must know about us coming. But before Tesla can step onto the bus, this little girl breaks through the barricade, runs up and hugs his leg. "Ahh. What's your name, little one?"
"Nikki. My mommy named me after you. She told me you made my home safe to live in."
Julie, I swear to God, I don't know how Tesla holds it together – tears start bursting out of my eyes. I'm such a sap. I mean, c'mon, Tesla literally saved all these lives. Every single person I see around me. But he just bends down, smiles, pats her on the head, and sends her off. "There you go. Back to your mommy."
So of course I can't help myself. As I hop on the bus, I turn to the crowd and shout "Hey! Anyone name their kid Chip?" And yeah, there's some cheering and shit, but no Chips. Oh well.

On the bus, Pete's still thinking about the name thing. "Clarence? Dude!"
"Yeah. Just never use it. Sorry I didn't tell you."
"No, I love it. Now when I get pissed at you I can be all *'Clarence... Clarence Chip Collins...'*"
"Great. When are you not pissed at me?"
He grins. "It happens."

From: Chip Collins
To: Julie Taylor
Date: June 4, 2015 5:43am
Re: Earth Fragment Five

Hi Julie,

He's perfect.

Don't get me wrong – I don't swing like that for my
alternates. But imagine meeting yourself – and he's like
the perfect version of you. In great shape, a glint in his eye,
a scar across his left cheek, badass uniform with badges
and guns all over the place. And a crew cut. That's what
Commander Clarence Collins looks like. G. I. Perfect Joe.

The only bad thing? It reminds me what a total slug I am.

Whatever. I walk up to him, and we smile that smile,
like meeting your long-lost twin, and shake hands.
"Commander! Dude! Can I call you Chip?"
His smile fades. "Actually, I dropped the Chip way back in
elementary school."
"But you still put a firecracker in Danny Boyle's
underpants, right?"
"Who's Danny Boyle?"
Uh oh. Shit's different. But he's cool. I mean he's me, right?
"So, uh, what should I call you?"
"Commander."

Wow. Kind of dickish. Strike one. But I let it slide. "Okay, Commander. So, can I ask? Julie? You know, *Julie*?"

"We're aware of Ms. Taylor from your journal entries with Mr. Tesla. But no Julie Taylor matching the specs on any Earth Fragment. Sorry. Good luck with that."

Strike two. This guy's got a fucking attitude. "Uh, hey. You can cut with the tough guy dick approach, dude. It's ME. Chip. We're alternates."

"Really? Well you can cut the slacker 'dude' approach, Chip. We've got work to do."

WTF? Could this possibly be a version of me? What happened, did Mom not hug him enough or something? So I go to give him a hug. And he backs up and gets in his *about-to-kick-my-ass* stance, and he's like "Woah. Do we have a problem?"

Huh. Not such a perfect version of me after all.

On our way to the briefing room, Pete can't help himself. He leans over and whispers "Dude. My alternate might report to yours, but yours is a dick."

"I know, right? I think Mom must have left him out in the rain or something."

"Yeah. He needs a few leg humps from Bobo."

Alternate Pete hears us talking and walks over. "Guys. You should cut Clarence some slack. He's actually a great guy. And he's got a lot on his plate. You know, with this whole Montrose thing."

"Who?"

"Yup."

"No, I said who. Who's Montrose?"

"Yup."

"Yup what?"

"Yup Who is Montrose."
"Now you're just repeating my question."
"WHO is Montrose."

Wait a second… I'm not getting stuck in the damn WHO loop again! "WHO is Montrose. Got it. I'm guessing that means Montrose is an alternate of WHO. But how do you guys know about all this? With WHO?"
"I'll let the Commander explain when we get to the briefing room."

Official Explanation of What The Fuck is Going On
By Commander Clarence Collins
(Kind of a Dick, But We're Told He's a Great Guy)
1. The journal. They used Tesla's journal not only to devise the antimatter collector and save the world by 1984, but continued to use it to follow our Tesla's journeys through parallel dimensions.
2. The ITA. Even though the Earth was shattered to pieces, the portal never moved. Once it was formed it occupied a fixed position in space. They logged its location, occasionally using the ITA for limited exploration for resources in other dimensions.
3. WHO. Once Tesla started writing to Chip about WHO and the prison, they've been tracking us, and waited for the opportune moment to save us from the clutches of WHO. (*Clutches* – God, I love that word.)
4. Montrose. WHO is human. He gave himself a name that can't be pronounced, like The Artist Formerly Known as Prince or some shit. Anyway, the folks on this dimension found his alternate!

And his name here? Bill Montrose. Yawn. Not very intimidating, Bill.

5. The plan. They're planning to use us, Tesla, and Bill Montrose (yawn) to battle WHO and once again save their world (and the rest of the multiverse in the process). How the fuck we're going to do that is anybody's guess.

Meg is skeptical (what else is new): "But isn't this Montrose person a killer then? If he's the alternate of WHO?" Alternate Pete fields the question. "You'd think. But what we've found is that, like the events in any particular dimension, people's personalities can be wildly different. One person can be kind, and their alternate can be cruel. So sure, WHO's a killer, but Montrose? Take a look for yourself."

He presses a button on the wall, and a big panel pulls back. From the shadows walks in a tall, hooded figure.

"WHO!"

Pete quickly stands in front of Meg, protecting her. Tesla quickly stands in front of the Bobos, protecting them. I quickly run for the door. (Hey, I don't want to lose the other foot!) Alternate Pete grabs my arm as I attempt my escape, smiles, and turns me around. And the figure pulls back his hood with a gentle laugh. "Ho, ho. Don't worry, folks. I'm with the good guys."

Holy shit. It's Santa all over again.

And this time it's not evil manipulative Santa! It's gentle, kind, benevolent Santa. "Santa?"

He laughs again. "No, afraid not. But I do have a gift for you. Commander, would you mind handing me that plant?"

I'm thinking *dying plant?* Gee thanks, dude. Nice Christmas gift. *Not.* But then Montrose holds up the plant and smiles at it.

The plant perks up instantly.

We're all entranced. It's that same whammy thing WHO did to me. This Montrose guy's got the same power over us. And obviously this plant.

"It's subtle. Plants react best to it."

The Commander takes the plant back and sets it down. "Okay, folks, so here's the quick: this person you're calling WHO, we believe he has the same power as Montrose here, but it manifests negatively, leading to death instead of life. We also believe he's devised an antimatter collector and amplifier from the schematics in your journal, Mr. Tesla, and is using it to amplify his ability. Once inside any universe, he can create a chain reaction, causing a total universe collapse."

Tesla can't contain himself. "The pages he ripped out of my journal! That mangy cur! I shall rip his still-beating heart from his chest and throw it to the dogs!"

I'm impressed. "Woah, Nikola! Didn't think you had it in you!"

"I apologize." He takes a deep breath. "Violence is never the solution. But he must be stopped."

The Commander puts both fists on the table. "Yes. Now enough talk. Let's get to work."

26
Five Minutes Without Shit Exploding

From: Chip Collins
To: Julie Taylor
Date: June 4, 2015 5:43am
Five minutes without shit exploding

Hi Julie,

Wow. It feels good to go five minutes without shit exploding, or running for your life, or having that weird feeling of being hungry and tired even though it's impossible to be hungry or tired in the ITA because time stands still.

Here it's different. Time passes. Food. Sleep. Man, you never really appreciate stuff until you go without. Nothing like an oversize cheeseburger and a shake, followed immediately by hours and hours of blissful slumber. Yeah. That shit rocks.

But waking up is tough. (I know, what else is new.) I'm just not a morning person, but that's my right, right? And these military people are all about waking up before the goddam rooster crows at like four-thirty in the morning.

Like this morning. They couldn't wait until eleven a.m. to get us fitted for our super-slick biker uniforms (which are awesome, btw.) It had to be oh-five-hundred pre-dawn o'clock, while I'm still dreaming of me and you going down that water slide at Wet'nWild, and we go flying into the sky like birds, and then we're in a big bright orange house, and there's literally an elephant in the middle of the room, and –

woah, man, that milkshake right before bed probably wasn't such a good idea.

So anyway we're in this training area getting poked and prodded, and I look over, and I can't help it. I see Pete and Meg whispering to each other.

She's crying a little. I feel bad.

"… and I'm excited by all this, it's beyond anything I could've imagined myself doing. I'm discovering things I wouldn't have discovered in an entire lifetime. It's not even that I'm scared. The danger is even exciting. I'm with you and that's wonderful. And Tesla! He's a dream."
"But?"
"But that's the problem. A *dream*. It doesn't feel *real*. There's this nagging feeling like I'm on hold. The time not passing in the hallway doesn't help. It's like real life will only start again when I'm home. Doesn't it feel the same for you?"
Pete nods. "Yes. Of course. But not exactly."
She's confused.
"Listen, it does feel unreal, but at the same time this is where I met you. And that's the most real thing I've had in a long time. So it's real. Here, let me prove how real it is."
He reaches over and pinches the skin on the back of her hand.
"Ouch! That hurt."
"It hurts because it's real."
I can see it, even from where I'm sitting two benches over. She wants to feel the same way. But she looks away.
"I promise, Meg. I'll get you home. If it's the last thing I do."
She half-smiles. "I know you will."

From: Chip Collins
To: Julie Taylor
Date: June 4, 2015 5:43am
Re: Five minutes without shit exploding

Hi Julie,

Knock-knock.

Knock-knock.

Knock-knock.

(This isn't a knock-knock joke. Somebody's annoying the crap out of me knocking on the door to my barracks room, while I'm half-naked, trying to wrestle my way out of this skin-tight fucking uniform.)

Knock-knock.

"What the fuck?! Enough! Go away!"
"Master Chip. It's me, Nikola."
I finally jerk the pants legs off me and fall over, banging my head on the corner of the end table. "Motherfucker!"
"Excuse me?"
"Not you! Hold on!"
I get up, stumble to the door, rubbing my poor noggin (how many bumps can one poor guy have on his head?), and open it. "What?"

Tesla's never seen me in my boxers, or probably *anybody* in their boxers, so he shields his eyes like he's looking directly at a white-hot nuclear blast. I close the door to a crack. "What?"

"Chip. I know this will seem petty, but the garments. I cannot – no, I *will* not – wear such a thing. It holds my body in embarrassing and uncomfortable ways I never imagined."

"I thought you'd be into that."

"You really thought I'd *'be into'* that?"

"Nah. Of course not. You're stuck in the forties. I get it. You got the one suit. Fits you like a glove. So why are you telling me? Go talk to our buddy Clarence."

"I did. He requested I talk to you."

"Huh. *Commander* Collins told you to talk to *me*? Okay. I'm not the boss of you. Wear whatever the fuck you want."

"Chip…"

"Whatever the *hell* you want."

"Chip!"

"Whatever the *berries* you want. I don't know. Wear whatever the *insert-favorite-non-swear-word-here* you want. Good night."

I close the door. Head to the bathroom.

Knock-knock.
Knock-knock.

I throw open the door. "Now what the fuck do you wa- oh, it's you."

Pete's looking around all top-secret-double-agent. "Pssst. You're not going to believe this. I just saw – hey! Are those my boxers? Dude - you've been wearing my boxers this whole time?"

"Okay, listen. Sorry. I was in your place, right before we left, and let's just say I wasn't exactly my freshest. So I'm like, hey we're taking a little day trip, I should be fresh and comfortable, right? How the hell was I supposed to know we'd be in the ITA for a million years? And what – you've never borrowed a pair of my boxers?"

"Are you fucking kidding?"

"Well have you?"

"No! Of course not! I don't want to smell like Chip ass! Speaking of which, where'd you put your old ones before we left? Do I even want to know?"

"In your hamper. Common courtesy when you borrow someone's boxers."

"Great. Now I'm going to have to burn the whole thing. I had like three dress shirts in there too."

"Dude. Chicks dig my aroma. Your shirts will be fine. In fact, they just appreciated in value. Anyway, drop it. What are you here for anyway? What did you just see that I won't believe?

"Oh. Right. It's Julie. She's here."

From: Chip Collins
To: Julie Taylor
Date: June 4, 2015 5:43am
Re: Five minutes without shit exploding

Hi Julie,

Yeah. I saw you last night.

You looked great. Red hair. Black biker suit. Like Black Widow from the Avengers. Walking outside the barracks. Me and Pete followed you.

So we're totally like a couple of high school kids pretending to be spies, stalking you from a distance, jumping from bush to bush. Yelling and punching each other but trying to be quiet about it.
"Shhhh!"
"You Shhhh! Why the fuck are you making so much noise?"
"Maybe it's your furry foot!"
"Why would a furry foot make noise? It's perfectly silent. That's just fucking mean!"
"You're right. Sorry. But it's not me. You're a klutz. You could never be a spy."
"I don't want to be a spy! I just want to get a good look at Julie without her see-"

"Hey. You guys okay?"

Whoops. So much for first impressions. There you are, (not you you, but Alternate You) standing over me and Pete while we're crouched in a wrestling hold behind a bush. Nice. Now that's how Alternate Julie will picture me for the rest of her life.

"I'm sorry. We just - I just, I thought I knew you."

"And you are?"

I stand up and shake off the dirt and leaves. "Chip. Chip Collins. This is my friend Pete."

"Huh. You look like the Commander. But I can't say I know you, either of you, sorry. And... could you stop looking at me like that?"

Julie, I'm an embarrassment. I must be doing the puppy dog eyes pretty bad, I can't even control myself. It's just been so long since I've seen you. It's incredible. You're back!

"Julie? It's you, right?"

"Sorry. Maureen. Okay, listen, Pete? Is that your name? You need to take your friend here back to his barracks. I think he's drunk."

And Pete's on it. He grabs me without a word and starts dragging me back home, while you walk away. I'm kicking and reaching back for you at this point – real classy-like. I'm surprised you didn't turn around and laugh.

"Julie! JULIE!" And then the tears come.

"Bwaaaahaaahaahahahaha!" (Imagine that's uncontrollable sobbing)

By now Pete's carrying me over his shoulder. "Dude. She's gone. And quit kicking me."

"No! I don't want to lose her! Not again!"

"Shhh. Dude, it's not her. I'm sorry. It's some girl Maureen. Same girl, but totally different. Who knows, her parents died when she was three and they moved to Idaho.

She doesn't know you. You never met. You know the drill.
Shit's crazy. It's not her."

"But…" and I'm lost again. I was so close to having you
back. "You don't know, man. You have somebody."

"Yeah. I have somebody. For now."

And I immediately stop crying and look at Pete. "Damn.
You okay dude?"

He shrugs. "Whatever. Can I put you down now without
you running away?"

27
The Epic Battle
for The Multiverse

From: Chip Collins
To: Julie Taylor
Date: June 4, 2015 5:43am
The epic battle for the multiverse (really, it's huge)

Hi Julie,

WHO is on the move. He's collapsing universes pretty
regularly now (it's easy to tell when – you feel like someone's
ripping your spine out of your body), and they've tracked
him to a dimension he must be using as a home base or
something. This place is buzzing with activity. Lots of
anticipation. Something's going to happen soon. But in the
meantime, here's a list of who's doing what:

Chip's Official List of Who's Been Doing What:
• Tesla and Meg have been helping the engineers from
Earth Fragment Five build a small, portable version of
the antimatter collector/amplifier that will fit through a
doorway to the ITA. I have no idea what they plan on doing
with it, or how it works, but it looks awesome. Like it could
definitely kick your ass sideways.
Check.

• Pete's been training with Alternate Pete's squadron on
battle tactics. God, he was born for this shit. Carry a big
gun, save the women and children, and look good while
you're doing it. It makes me tired just thinking about it, but
good for him.
Check.

• Montrose is barely around. I imagine they've got him in some secret room, using his Jedi powers to raise a nice tomato garden or something. I mean the guy literally wouldn't hurt a fly, so I don't know how he's going to beat up the bad guys. But I'm glad he's on our side anyway. Check.

• The Bobos have been hanging with me mostly, just being funny some of the time, and going into their mini-coma states the rest of the time. We have little dance contests, and of course they always win. Every once in a while, I'll look straight into one of their eyes, looking for some deep message, but all I get is blink-blink, or *"BEEZNEEZ,"* or *"ASSGAS."* (They like doing that last one because it cracks me up every time.)
Anyway, Check.

• Me? I guess they figured I was more harm than good, so they let me do whatever the hell I want. And don't get me wrong – I'm *loving* it. Sleep in, video games, lunch, dance party with the Bobos, go get a smoothie, party with the officers, mounch, crash, repeat.
Check.

So anyway this morning we get an announcement:
"All personnel report to field three."

Sounds pretty casual, right? Like it's a pickup game of hoops. So everyone, probably around five hundred biker-suit-clad military types (but not Alternate Julie/Maureen, I notice – she probably asked for a transfer to Earth Fragment Whichever-One-Is-Farthest-Away-From-That-Chip-Guy), they make their way to the big open field off to the south of the barracks.

The Commander's on a little platform with a microphone. "All right people – the scouts have returned with new intel. WHO is planning an attack on this dimension, within forty-eight hours. He's got an antimatter amplifier, and several hundred troops. We've got the manpower and the artillery to match that. So we're taking the fight to him first. Starting now."

So much for casual. Everyone starts murmuring really loud, getting antsy. I'm playing it cool, because of course I knew something like this was coming. (Kidding. I'm practically shitting myself in terror.)

"Before you report to your stations, though, I'd like to invite someone up to say a few words. Someone with valuable experience inside the Interdimensional Transfer Apparatus. Someone who, I've learned, has applied smarts, savvy, courage, and leadership in traveling the ITA, rescuing Mr. Tesla, and confronting WHO…"

Cool. I get to hear Pete make a speech. This is gonna rock.

"…Chip Collins."

What the hell? I shake my head politely and point to Pete. No thank you. Nope. Pete's your man. But the Commander's pretty insistent, and people are looking at me, waiting. Oh, what the hell. I jump up on the platform.

"Hey, people of Earth Fragment Five. Of all the remaining fragments of Earth. Now I'm not known for talking a lot, but I'll give it a go." (Pete does that thing where you cough really loud and say "BULLSHIT!" at the same time. So I give him the finger, and of course the Bobos jump up on the platform too and start giving the finger to the crowd, their message of universal peace, and all the seriousness and solemnity of the moment goes out the window. But I forge on. I mean, how many times do I get the mic in front of five hundred people?)

"Anyway, what we've seen, Pete and myself, and Nikola, and Meg, and even my two strange friends here Bobo and Bobo, what we've seen is incredible.
Unbelievable.
And yes, I've seen a great evil in the multiverse. Evil that must be stopped.
But we will stop it.
You know how I know?
Because I've seen other things, too.
I've seen an old man work his entire life to light the world.
I've seen friends willing to die for each other.
I've seen two people fall in love in the middle of chaos.
I've seen sacrifice, and courage, and humor in the lowest moments.
I've seen the brightest of light.
And this light will never go out. No evil, no darkness, no shadow can live in that light for long.
We will prevail. We will prevail, because we hold that light in our hearts."

Wow. Where the hell did that come from? These are battle-ready fighters, and they're wiping back tears and cheering. And I know what Pete's thinking: "Is that the same Chip that stole my boxers?"

Tesla inches his way up to the platform. The crowd hushes. He pats me on the head and winks at me, then turns to the mic. "I think what master Chip is trying to say is... Let us kick some buttocks!"

The troops erupt in the loudest laughter and cheering I've ever heard. And I swear, Julie, it'll suck if all this is for nothing, if it all ends now and I never get to see you again – but at that moment?

I actually became the perfect version of myself.

I lean over to Commander Collins. "Thanks for that, sir."
He smiles. "I've learned a lot about you from the others. I'm impressed. And proud."
"So... can I call you Chip now?"
"Don't get ahead of yourself."

From: Chip Collins
To: Julie Taylor
Date: June 4, 2015 5:43am
Re: The epic battle for the multiverse (really, it's huge)

Hi Julie,

So imagine this: You've got like a battalion of army guys, ships, weapons, all this huge gear – and it all has to fit through a twenty-eight-inch-wide doorway.

Okay, now stop imagining that. That's not what happens. Commander Collins might have dickish tendencies, but he's not an idiot. So his plan: take small teams through the ITA, all sneaky-like into WHO's dimension, set up secret camps overnight, and storm his base in the morning with hundreds of trained fighters (and Pete). Me, Meg, Tesla and the Bobos will be bringing up the rear, and won't see any action. Thank God.

Oops. Our team's up next. Gotta go. Wish me luck.

From: Chip Collins
To: Julie Taylor
Date: June 4, 2015 5:43am
Re: The epic battle for the multiverse (really, it's huge)

Hi Julie,

Something's not right.

I can't think straight, and it's dark. So dark all I can see is
the phone screen.

There's a lot of screaming.

I'm scared, babe.

From: Chip Collins
To: Julie Taylor
Date: June 4, 2015 5:43am
Re: The epic battle for the multiverse (really, it's huge)

Hi Julie,

Somebody's dragging me. Dragging me back into the hallway.

"You stay put. Take care of Tesla."

It's Commander Collins. Or what's left of him. He's bleeding real bad. Limping. Looks like he's missing a foot. Ironic.

He plops me next to a row of other bodies: Tesla, Meg, Alternate Pete, some others. Not sure who's alive or dead. One of the Bobos is here, rocking back and forth, hugging his knees. The Commander turns to head back through the ITA into WHO's dimension.

"Wait. What happened?"

"They knew we were coming. Dammit. They picked us off in the middle of the night. And we were wrong about several hundred. There's just too many of them. Thousands. Tens of thousands. And WHO's antimatter amplifier is too powerful. A handful of us are left, protecting Montrose. Gotta go."

I try to get up, my head nearly splitting open with pain.
"Wait. I'm coming."
"No you're not. You stay here. When you're ready to move,
take Tesla and any other survivors back to our dimension."
I struggle to my feet. "What. So we can die there?"
The Commander just looks at me like he doesn't need my
shit at the moment. Then he sighs. He understands. "Okay.
You sure you're ready for this?"

He opens the doorway.

And Julie, it's like Lord of the Fucking Rings in this
dimension – a giant battle field, strewn with bodies. Rubble
everywhere, the New Yorker hotel is long gone, shit, most
of New York City is long gone. Fire everywhere. Darkness.
Plasma machine guns going off left and right. Screaming.

This place is literally hell.

Out of the corner of my eye, I see Pete. He's firing some big
gun at WHO's minions, him and a bunch of our fighters are
circled around Montrose. Maybe a hundred and fifty people
left, max. And Montrose is standing there, hooked up to
this antimatter amplifier (there's a couple of what looks like
IVs going from the machine right into his arms), all calm
and serene, concentrating, with his hand over a big red
metal button. Pete screams over to him. "Montrose! Another
pulse in 3… 2… 1…"

And I finally get to see what this antimatter thing does.

Holy shit.

Montrose smacks the button, and this blast of light explodes in every direction for probably a mile, even coming into the open doorway me and the Commander are standing in.

But it doesn't destroy anything. For a mile around, anybody it reaches sort of stops what they're doing. They put down their guns. Look around at each other like "what the hell am I doing here? And what's this gun for?" It's like a little circle of heaven in the middle of hell. I guess Montrose didn't have to kick any ass after all.

But it's not enough.

From the other end of the field of rubble, north, maybe around where 59th street should be, comes another blast. But this one's totally black. And big. It envelopes everything for miles.

The Commander slams the doorway shut just before the blast reaches us. "That's WHO. You don't want to get hit with that. Look."

He reopens the door a crack, and everyone I just saw, all sort of peaceful, has been knocked on their asses, and is getting up, mad with rage, grabbing their guns and running back into battle. Anyone that's wounded looks like they've died. (Pete's team looks okay though. Some kind of protective bubble from Montrose I'm guessing.) Anyway, he's back to shooting whatever he can to protect Montrose.

Julie, I'm not kidding. The battle for the multiverse is literally a battle between light and darkness. And darkness is knocking light's lights out. (Lights lights? Remind me to think of a better metaphor next time.)

"It's been going on like that all night. We can't gain any ground. There are too many of-"
Something whizzes by my ear, right into his chest.
"Commander!"
He falters to his knees, looking down at the object sticking out from between his ribs. "Fuck."
"Holy shit. It's a *Shogun*."
"What the hell is a *Shogun*?"
"That. Sticking out of your chest."
"Right. Got any ideas?"
"Yeah. Don't touch any of the buttons."

As I reach down for button five (the one that either does nothing or disengages this thing), a jolt of electricity from the Shogun hurls me back ten feet, and sends the Commander to the floor.

More darkness.

From: Chip Collins
To: Julie Taylor
Date: June 4, 2015 5:43am
Re: The epic battle for the multiverse (really, it's huge)

When I wake up, I look over to the Commander. He's not moving, laying right in the doorway, half in the ITA, half in hell. I rush over to him. "Commander. Chip. Hold on, dude. Hold on."
He stirs. "….chip?"
"I'm here."
"…chip …i never told you…"
I'm freaking out. "No, don't do this! Don't do the *I-never-told-you* thing! Get up so we can get back to Montrose. There's work to do! Come on!"
"…i never told you …you're actually not a bad looking guy…"
I laugh through my tears. "Get up, dude! Time to go."
He smiles, wipes my cheek. "…don't cry …there are infinite versions of us… I'm just one… of infinite chips… we'll fight to the very last one…"

And he dies. Right there in my arms.

I'm beating his chest, screaming, crying. It's over. It's over. It's over. Time to give up. There's just too many of the bad guys. Too many of them. Bobo is tugging at my shirt sleeve. He keeps tugging. Tugging. Go away, Bobo.

Wait.
Bobo.
Too many of them…
Infinite Chips…
We'd win this battle if we had infinite Chips.
But where do you get infinite Chips?
Wait.
Not infinite Chips.
Bobo.

That's it.

I lay Commander Clarence "Chip" Collins gently next to Tesla and Meg, turn to Bobo and bend down. I look deep into those eyes, and ask him with my mind, "are you thinking what I'm thinking?"

Bobo nods. And his mind message back to me is loud and clear:

BOBO ARMY.

From: Chip Collins
To: Julie Taylor
Date: June 4, 2015 5:43am
Re: The epic battle for the multiverse (really, it's huge)

I grab Bobo and we jump through the doorway into hell, sprinting over to the last remaining group of fighters and Montrose. The sounds of fighting are deafening. I grab Pete's shoulder.

"Pete!"

He swerves around, almost shooting us. "Dude! What the fuck! Get the hell out of here!"

"Give me a grenade!"

"What?!"

"Give me a grenade!"

"No! Now get the fuck out of here! Go help Meg!"

I don't have the heart to tell him Meg's laying in the hallway, lifeless. And I don't have time to argue with him about a fucking grenade. I reach over and grab one from his belt, and stuff it into Bobo's mouth. Bobo pulls me down to his eye level – he's got one more message.

THANKS DUDE.

And he swallows the grenade whole. And winks at me. (Wow - where the hell did he learn to do that?) Then he's off, running like a tiny little madman, to get as far away from us as possible before the blas-

SSSSSPPPLLLLAAAATTTTT!!!!

Ewww. He didn't quite make it far enough. Me and Pete and the others are covered in little pieces of Bobo. Ick.

Pete doesn't even know what to say. He's stammering. "What- what- what- what…" He's in shock, swaying back and forth. He thinks I've lost my mind. The last insane moments of his desperate, idiot friend.

I reach over and steady him. "Pete. Dude. Trust me." And sure enough, Julie, sure enough, the little pieces of Bobo start moving, start growing, and in a few minutes… little teeny-tiny one-foot-tall Bobos all over the place! It's hilarious!

Pete's eyes widen with understanding. "Chip, you're a fucking genius!" And he turns to the rest of the group. "Everyone! Give your grenades to the Bobos!"

So for the next hour, little Bobos are running forward, blowing themselves up, creating more Bobos, until the field ahead of us is filled to overflowing with furry aliens, biting and kicking and smothering everything in their path.

Tens of thousands of Bobos! Imagine the leg humping!

Pete sees we're making headway. "Okay, dude. Go get the Commander and Alternate Pete. I need orders." I look at him and shake my head. "Can't. Gone." Pete's speechless again. He can't move. Montrose lifts his head from the amplifier. "Chip and Pete. Your friends have passed. We will mourn them later. But you are here. Here to lead us to our destiny. Now we march on WHO!"

And instantly, like Moses at the Red Sea, the nearly infinite sea of Bobos parts for us.

Watch out, WHO. Here we come.

From: Chip Collins
To: Julie Taylor
Date: June 4, 2015 5:43am
Re: The epic battle for the multiverse (really, it's huge)

Hi Julie,

Well, it's quite a sight.

Me, Pete, this oversize guy who looks like Santa hooked up to an antimatter amplifier, fifty or so battle-weary soldiers, and about a million Bobos are all marching up Eighth Avenue, or whatever's left of it.

We've knocked out WHO's army, and Pete and team are taking out any stragglers. It's quiet. Montrose's light blasts have been protecting us from WHO's black blasts of death. So of course, when we get there, up to Columbus Circle, we're expecting WHO to be cowering in a corner, clutching his teddy bear and whimpering.

But he's laughing. Motherfucker's laughing. Again.

And now that we're close enough, he hits us with the whammy. Our whole group, even the first few rows of Bobos, get stuck in his trance. "Well, hello boys and girls. I thought you'd never get here. But don't worry – I kept myself busy tidying up the place."

The entire scene is black. Black rubble, black sky, black dust hanging in the air, black– well, you get the picture. Very black. I think he's being sarcastic. But if he was going for monochromatic dreariness, he nailed it.

"And you've brought my brother! How thoughtful!" WHO and Montrose lock eyes. They smile at each other. But in those eyes you can see a battle being waged, a terrible battle of good versus evil. Light versus darkness. Hulk Hogan versus The Undertaker (okay, maybe just two comparisons was enough).

Montrose speaks first. "If you are my brother, then put down your weapons, and declare this a day of peace." WHO laughs again. "Brother. Brother. You know I was joking, right? You are not my brother. You are a version of me, who I might have been, given the possibility. But I no longer give possibilities. I take them away!" WHO slams his fist onto the button of his amplifier, and we're so close, that even with Montrose's protective bubble of light, the blast knocks all of us, and the swarm of Bobos, back about twenty feet. I look back at Montrose – he's unhooked from the amplifier, breathing heavy, closing his eyes. Our protective bubble disappears. Uh oh. We're fucked.

"Well, *'brother.'* It looks like I'm about to become an only child." He raises his hand to the button again. "Goodby- "

And he freezes.

WHO's whammy stops. He's got something sticking out of his neck. Pete whips around to see where it came from.

It was me.

For just a moment, I had shaken off WHO's whammy, seen clearly what needed to be done. He would not have power over me. Not now. This moment was mine. (Remember that Shogun that killed the Commander? Well I pulled it out of his body, thinking it might come in handy. And boy, it sure did.) I hurled it at WHO in that short moment. And stopped him. Yes, that's right ladies and gentlemen...

Chip Collins, *Shogun* Master!

The wicked old witch is dead. Oz is safe again.
Me and Pete start high-fiving, jumping up and down.
Everyone starts hugging and cheering.

"We did it! We saved the multiverse!"

But then Montrose groans. Oh shit. Almost forgot about him. We rush over to his side.
"Friends... no time to celebrate... he... is not like you..."
And sure enough, by the time we look back, WHO's standing there, unfrozen and smiling. He reaches up, pulls the Shogun out of his neck with a gush of blood (gross), and laughs. Then he hurls it at us. It hits Montrose right in the temple.

Montrose lets out a final groan and goes silent.

"As I was saying, goodbye dear brother. Now, if you'll excuse me, I've got universes to collapse."
He's gloating. What a dick. He even pulls out this pinky ball from his coat and shows it to us.

"A pinky ball?"

"It's not a *pinky ball*, Chip, you imbecile, whatever that is. This is what I use to collapse universes. You can thank your friend Nikola for the design – if he's still alive. It's the Reverse Baryogenesis Device."

"Reverse Barywhat?"

"Baryogenesis. It recreates the dangerous imbalance of baryons and antibaryons produced in the early univer– you know what? Look it up on Wikipedia, Chip. I don't have time to explain. I just wanted you all to see it before I killed you. Amazing little thing, isn't it?"

"Doesn't look too amazing to me. Where's the button?"

WHO laughs. "Buttons! Ha! Buttons, buttons. Everything's got to have buttons. You've got a lot to learn, boy. All I have to do is hold this between my palms like so…" and he demonstrates for me.

The pinky ball – or baryogenewhatever – starts glowing.

"Oh dear…"

WHO looks like he just knocked over his mother's favorite vase, and it crashed into a million pieces, and her car's pulling up the driveway. He just accidentally started a universe collapse. His own universe. What an idiot. He's fucked.

Wait. We're all fucked.

"RUN!!!" (God, do you realize how many times we've had to run for our lives? Enough. If I ever get home, I'm never running again.)

Thirty blocks or so to the ITA. I don't know what a universe collapse looks like, but we better get a move on!

We all start running. Pete, me, the other fighters, and WHO's right behind us. Around us, it's hard to describe, but you can sort of see the fabric of the scene come apart. Like we're inside a TV show, and somebody's pulling the plug on the set. (I'm guessing WHO usually does this while he's standing right in the doorway of the ITA, not a quarter mile away.)

I turn around to see how close WHO is. And suddenly the Bobos surround him. Imagine ten thousand Bobos swarming around you. WHO's in for a world of hurt. Good for him. I'm done with him.

Okay. Thanks, Bobos. Now onto the ITA.

A MILLION HOURS LATER...

I can see it. Another fifty yards. We're gonna make it.

But the ground beneath us starts to dissolve. It's just not there – it's disappearing. My feet try to move forward, but it's like running in quicksand. Pete's up ahead a yard or two, looking back, we're all frantically trying to reach the goddamn doorway. It's right there! Come ON!

And then the universe gives way and I'm falling.

From: Chip Collins
To: Julie Taylor
Date: June 4, 2015 5:43am
Re: The epic battle for the multiverse (really, it's huge)

Hi Julie,

Well, this is it.

Here I am, not falling anymore, just sort of floating in nothingness.

It's kind of peaceful. So this is what it's like to die.

At least we took WHO down with us. Stupid motherfucker.

I look up at Pete, he made it a little closer to the doorway, but still not enough. He looks down at me. And he smiles. He's calm. "Dude, it's over."
"Yeah, it's over."
"But we did it. We actually DID something. If you hadn't talked me into this stupid shit, we wouldn't have saved the multiverse. Do you know what that means?"
"You're not pissed about the boxers anymore?"
"No. It means that this is all because of you."
"But we're done. Dead."
"Yeah. But Meg might be alive up top. And Tesla. And Julie's definitely alive. And our families are alive. And everyone else we care about. And everyone that *everyone* cares about. Everywhere. You did that." He takes my hand in the nothingness. "Thanks."

I look down at our hands. They're becoming transparent. We're disappearing.

"Now go ahead and say your goodbyes to Julie. I'll wait. I'm not going anywhere."

Right. Julie.

Okay, babe, I've got one last thing to tell you before I go. I know you'll never read this, but if you think of me ever, take a second to remember what we had, so maybe at least it'll be written down in the Great Book of Life before it disappears forever.

Remember that time the bike messenger crashed into you, and you were crying on the ground, and I carried you home four blocks.

Remember when you got that tattoo and the guy misspelled "their," and instead of killing him, you laughed and said "maybe their right" and we bought you a long-sleeve shirt to cover it up.

Remember the time we went to that halloween party dressed as Mary Kate and Ashley Olsen, and nobody knew who we were, and you had to put out the fire on my wig.

Remember that time your ice cream cone flopped onto your shoe, and I picked it up and ate it anyway, and gave you mine.

Remember the time-

Wait... is that a rope?

From: Chip Collins
To: Julie Taylor
Date: June 4, 2015 5:43am
Re: The epic battle for the multiverse (really, it's huge)

Hi Julie,

A rope! Holy shit!

I grab hold, and look up – Pete and the dozen fighters
above us are dangling in the nothingness, from a rope. It's
coming out of the doorway. Who's that at the top?

Tesla!

And next to him – Meg! They're both alive!

Slowly, they pull maybe a dozen survivors, into the doorway.
Pretty soon everyone's helping Pete, and then I'm last.

I'm saved! I'm alive! It's over!

"Chip! Look out!"

Fuck. It's not over. I look behind me down the rope.
And I don't know how, it's impossible, but you guessed
it: douchebag WHO is climbing the rope after me.
Goddammit. And then he tries the whammy on me again.

I can hear him whisper. "Chip. It's too bad about your Bobo friends. They just didn't have it in them. My trance worked especially well on their feeble minds. But you? You've got that fighting spirit. I like that. I could use a boy like you."

NO.
I will not look back. I will not get sucked into your mind, you evil dick. Never again. I climb closer to the doorway. "Chip. I have Julie. Help me into the hallway and I'll let you talk to her."
I hesitate. Could he? Could he really have you? I wonder. "Can I see her?"

But before WHO can answer, a hand grabs me through the doorway. It's Pete. He pulls me a few feet into the hallway and smacks me. "Dude! Dude! Wake up!"
Whew. I'm in the ITA. "Thanks, dude."

We turn around. In the doorway, WHO's fingers (on the hand he still has) are grabbing frantically for a grip. Tesla stands above him in the doorway, looking a bit like he doesn't know what to do.

The universe behind WHO is almost gone. The last little wisps of light are disappearing, and WHO is getting more and more transparent. He's almost gone, too.

He smiles and whispers to Tesla. "You and I, Nikola, we can do this together. Help me through the doorway. We can share dominion over the multiverse. Don't you want to step out of the shadows, my good man, and into the light?" Tesla answers. "What do you know of light?" And together, we all step behind him, Pete, and Meg, and me, and the others, and we put our hands on his shoulders, and look down at WHO.

The next few seconds seem to last forever. WHO looks up at Tesla, at us. We have created something he never could, not with a million antimatter amplifiers, or a million baryogenewhatevers. He could have defeated us today, and gone on collapsing universes forever, and still he couldn't win. Because there is something about the beings in the multiverse, something that binds them, something invincible, that can never be extinguished. Light. And he knows for the first time.

"...I have seen it... finally..."

He lets go of his grip, and disappears into nothingness.

WHO is gone.

The door slams shut and immediately vanishes. Just an empty spot of wall where a doorway used to be.

It's the last universe to collapse.

And in the next moment, a doorway reappears in the same spot. The multiverse has spawned a new possibility. Infinity is back. Good. I like infinity.

Me, Pete, Tesla, and Meg all hug each other. For a long time. We cry for the Bobos, and for Commander Collins and Alternate Pete, for Montrose, and all the people lost in the fight. We cry out of relief, of knowing somehow, incredibly, miraculously, we did it. We saved the multiverse.

Tesla's the first to speak. "Dear friends. Let's go home."

28
Home

From: Chip Collins
To: Julie Taylor
Date: June 4, 2015 5:43am
Home

Hi Julie,

HOME.

My favorite word.

I can say it now, and actually believe it.

Julie, I'm coming home. I'll be there soon.

WHO's gone. Everybody who survived is patched up.
We've got our hands on an INTERDIMENSIONAL
NAVIGATION CONTROLLER (typed that out in all caps
for you, Nikola). So the going's easy.

First, we drop off the folks from Earth Fragment Five. There
are the funerals, of course. It's super sad. But there's also
a cool feeling of unity – like somehow, people from across
dimensions, alternates of themselves, came together to
protect the fabric of the multiverse. To protect the beauty of
possibility, of infinite choices. To protect the-

"Dude. Who the fuck are you talking to?"
"Huh? Nobody. Just thinking about everything."

"Well, I know it's new for you, but stop thinking for a minute. We're here."

And there we are. At the doorway to Meg's dimension. This time it's Pete sniffing back tears. Meg's got her hand on the latch to the door. She's trying to be the strong one now. He won't let her go.
"Pete, it breaks my heart, but this is the right thing to do."
"Well it doesn't feel right."

Pete enters the combination, and together they turn the latch. Shwoosh.

I jump over and put my hand on theirs, and shove the door closed.

"Wait. Pete. Why don't you go with her? We left a mess back there with BOK and everything. She's going to need a superhero like The Brute to watch out for her."
"No. I-"
"I'll be fine."
"No. I belong-"
"No. You belong with Meg. Dude, I said it before – you've carried me for a long time. But look how far I've come. I can do this on my own. Plus, I have this." I point down to the INController. "I can visit you guys anytime you need Awesome Man."
He laughs. "What about home?"
"I'll take care of your place."
"I bet you will. This was probably your plan all along – lure Pete into the ITA and steal his apartment."
"Yup. And I'll tell everybody you're on some kind of wild adventure with a skinny girl with a PhD from far away.

And I won't be lying."

Meg smiles. "Pete, you know, I think Chip's got another genius idea there."

I punch him in the shoulder. "And you can come home any time you want to visit, you idiot."

Pete grabs me in a bear hug. He won't let go. "Okay. But who's going to fuck up my life from now on?"

"Maybe Meg's up to the task. Who knows what crazy shit she can get you into with her brain, your brawn, and a safe deposit box stuffed with a hundred thousand dollars?" And I let go of Pete, and give Meg a kiss on the cheek.

And Pete and Meg walk through the doorway (without anyone hitting their head for once) into whatever waits for them on the other side.

Goodbye, Pete.

From: Chip Collins
To: Julie Taylor
Date: June 4, 2015 5:43am
Re: Home

Hi Julie,

Now it's just me and Nikola Tesla.

Pete has decided to follow his love. Good for him. He deserves all good things and more.

And after what seems like an eternity (in a way it has been, right?), we finally stop in front of our door.

Home.

Dimension #234,698,594,394,683.

"Hey Nikola. How'd you come up with that number? Does it have some kind of cosmic significance or something?"
"No. Completely arbitrary. I simply like that number. I think it's my favorite."
"My favorite number is eleven."
"Oh, Chip, that reminds me."
"Yeah?"
"We need to go in separately."
"No way. Together."

"You don't understand. If we go in together, we will create a paradox. The ITA will try to place me back in January 7, 1943, and place you in June 4, 2015. A paradox."

"And paradox is bad."

"Very bad. The opposite of *berries*."

"Really? I was imagining us growing old together. Well, me growing old, and you, ah, I don't know. Fuck. This is terrible. I wanted you to meet Julie."

"Tell her any time she uses electricity, that we've met. In a way." Aww. That was cute. But dammit. I guess this is it. Fucking guy grew on me. I really am going to miss him. Almost as much as Pete. But no more tears. Enough. I point to the door. "Go ahead, Nikola. Age before beauty."

Tesla laughs. And one last time, he bends down a little, and musses up my hair. "Chip. It has been my honor and privilege to travel the multiverse with you. You have shown not only great courage, but keen resourcefulness, and unwavering loyalty to your friends. I have never met anyone quite like you."

"Aww. I'm blushing."

"You should be. I am lucky to have had you in my life. Goodbye, master Chip. God bless your journeys. And say hello to Julie for me. I'm certain you'll make a wonderful couple. And Chip?"

"Yeah?"

"Try, try not to swear so much."

"Fuck that. KIDDING! I'm kidding! Okay, Nikola, I'll give it a shot. Promise."

We hug, and God, I could break him in two, he's so old and I'm so broken up. But I finally let him go, and he steps back into 1943.

Goodbye, Nikola Tesla.

From: Chip Collins
To: Julie Taylor
Date: June 4, 2015 5:43am
Re: Home

Hi Julie,

And now it's my turn.

Alone in the hallway, I stare at the door. The rest of my life starts on the other side of that door. The rest of my life with you. I hope.

I love you, Julie. Now more than ever. I can't wait to see you.

I'm home.

I enter the magical numbers 0-0-0-0 one last time, turn the latch, hear the shwoosh, and walk through the doorway.

And yes, I hit my head.

From: Chip Collins
To: Everyone
Date: June 7, 2015 2:44pm
Re: Home

Hey reader person,

If you're the kind of reader who likes to leave the ending all ambiguous, like "I wonder what happens to Chip and Julie?" stop reading right now. Close the book or your kindle or iPad or whatever shit (whoops, sorry Nikola) they're reading on these days. Enjoy pondering it for yourself, just lay down your head, you've come to journey's end, and dream of the story that's been told, and imagine the future.

If you're NOT that kind of reader, if you want to know all the juicy details and have it all wrapped up in a big giant red bow like me, read on!

- Chip

From: Chip Collins
To: Everyone
Date: June 7, 2015 2:44pm
Re: Home

Hey reader person (the kind who wants to know what happened),

So as soon as I walk through the doorway, my phone starts buzzing like crazy. I look down.

NOW SENDING 3,612 EMAILS

Holy shit. 3,612 emails. I hope Julie's inbox can take that many.

Dashing down to the lobby, I take a moment to hug the Manager, and Miss Barber behind the counter, and people are looking at me like I'm nuts. But I'm George Bailey from *It's a Wonderful Life* right now, or Scrooge on Christmas morning, jumping up and down and loving every beautiful moment of my own dimension - HOME!

I'M HOME! I'M HOME! I'M HOME!

I'm even wishing everyone Merry Christmas in June. I don't care. It's awesome.

I run to Julie's apartment (not at a bad pace either – I hate running, but all this crazy shit has gotten me into some decent shape finally), and you can imagine the soundtrack playing behind me, rousing trumpets and french horns and violins and shit, announcing the hero's return to his love. Animated bluebirds are practically following me, this is so sweet.

Finally. Her door. Another door. Another choice.

Am I ready? Am I worthy?

While my hand hovers on the door thinking about knocking, she answers.

Julie.

Wow. I've heard people talk about really experiencing the "now," how when you really dive into it, the present moment, that everything gets a little halo around it, the beauty of it all sort of glows. I thought it was bullshit. But it's true. She's glowing. Her beautiful red hair. Her Spongebob t-shirt. Her cute little feet in those ratty flip-flops that she won't throw away. It's all glowing.

She looks at me, startled. Then she smiles.

I smile back. This is awesome.

Then she punches me in the face.

From: Chip Collins
To: Everyone
Date: June 7, 2015 2:44pm
Re: Home

"So is this another one of your stupid jokes? Sending me three thousand emails?"

Ouch. My nose is bleeding. Should I tell her I have even more handwritten letters wadded up in my pocket?

"You disappear for two months, not a word, then I get a bunch of horse shit from you all at once. You know what? You're an asshole. I don't care if you send me five thousand-"

I grab her and kiss her. And this time, it really is the longest kiss ever. Pete would tell us to get a room. I'm crying, and laughing, and hugging her, and kissing every inch of her face.

Julie pulls back. She searches my eyes.

"Chip. Are you all right?"
"I am now."

And Julie takes my hand, and pulls me into her apartment, and closes the door.

From: Ted Swanson, FBI
To: Chip Collins
Date: June 12, 2015 7:12pm
Your Employment

Dear Mr. Collins,

You're fired.

In addition to not bothering to show up at work since
June 4, you left a giant desk and papers all over the place.
I'm keeping your screwdriver.

I don't know how you even got this job. Wait, yes I do.
Somebody up top got a recommendation letter for you. All
very official, through Western Union. How'd you swing that
one? In fact, by law I have to let you read it. But you're still
fired.

> Dear sirs,
>
> I understand that a young man named
> Chip Collins will be seeking employment
> as a security guard for the FBI research
> facility in Queens, New York. I would
> like to recommend him for this position.
>
> Why? Let me just say I've known master
> Chip for quite a while, and he is special.

He is a friend. And a teacher. And a
leader. In fact, he is one in infinity.

And he is needed in that position. Trust
me.

Respectfully,
- Nikola T.

P.S. If Chip should inquire about obtaining
a desk, it's safe to say we'll all be better
off if you grant his request.

From: Pete Turner
To: Chip Collins
Date: October 23, 2015 1:04am
Dude

Dude,

You still have your Awesome Man cape laying around?
I could use a hand.

- Pete

Afterword
About Nikola Tesla

This is a work fiction. But it's inspired by the fantastic and strange story of Nikola Tesla, one of the greatest inventors and visionaries ever.

Tesla, born in 1856 in Austria, was a Serbian-American inventor, electrical engineer, mechanical engineer, physicist, and futurist best known for his contributions to the design of the modern alternating current (AC) electricity supply system.

He gained experience in telephony and electrical engineering before emigrating to the United States in 1884 to work for Thomas Edison in New York City. He soon struck out on his own with financial backers, setting up laboratories and companies to develop a range of electrical devices. His patented AC induction motor and transformer were licensed by George Westinghouse, who also hired Tesla as a consultant to help develop a power system using alternating current.

Tesla is also known for his high-voltage, high-frequency power experiments in New York and Colorado Springs which included patented devices and theoretical work used in the invention of radio communication, for his X-ray experiments, and for his ill-fated attempt at intercontinental wireless transmission in his unfinished Wardenclyffe Tower project.

Tesla's achievements and his abilities as a showman demonstrating his seemingly miraculous inventions made him world-famous. Although he made a considerable amount of money from his patents, he spent a lot on numerous experiments. He lived for most of his life in a series of luxury New York hotels, although the end of his patent income and eventual bankruptcy led him to live in less elaborate circumstances. Tesla continued to invite the press to parties he held on his birthday to announce new inventions he was working on and make (sometimes unusual) public statements. Because of his pronouncements and the nature of his work over the years, Tesla gained a reputation in popular culture as the archetypal "mad scientist." He died on January 7, 1943.

Popular memory of Tesla and his work declined after his death, but since the 1980s his reputation has experienced a resurgence in popular culture. Tesla, indeed, lives on.

Source: Wikipedia, 2015

You've finished.
Please review this book on Amazon.com!

One of the best ways for independent authors and small publishers to get exposure for their books is to receive as many honest, thoughtful reviews as possible.

Thanks in advance!

About Rob Dircks

Rob Dircks is and has been many things - author, advertising agency owner, aspiring screenwriter, stock video director and producer, iPhone app developer, photographer, and more (and yes, even a security guard in college). He lives in New York with his wife Kellie and two kids. You can read more about him and get in touch at www.robdircks.com.

More Books from Rob
Okay, there's only one. But it's a doozy:

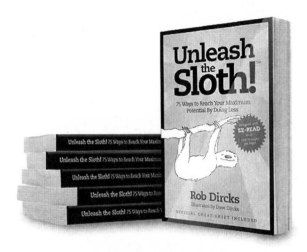

Unleash The Sloth!
75 Ways to Reach Your Maximum
Potential By Doing Less

Available at amazon.com, through the iTunes store,
and at www.unleashthesloth.com.

It's the self-help book you've always wanted. The one that tells
you're fine just the way you are – and that you can probably
get away with doing even less. It sounds like a paradox, I
know. But just look at the mighty sloth, who makes no excuses
for who he is – and becomes everything he needs to be.

And now it's your turn. Take a nap instead of mowing
the lawn. Save yourself a few steps and jaywalk. Save
yourself a few pen strokes and replace your signature with
an X. Make life easier, and you'll find that you'll be just as
lovable, productive or unproductive as you would've been
anyway – but without all the unnecessary stress and guilt.

Now THAT'S what I call reaching your potential!

GOLDFINCH 🦅 PUBLISHING

About
Goldfinch Publishing™

Goldfinch Publishing is a boutique publishing house
created to facilitate the shift from traditional to independent
publishing. We do this by offering professional curation
(Goldfinch Select), paid services (Goldfinch A La Carte),
and free information and resources (Goldfinch DIY).

www.goldfinchpublishing.com

CPSIA information can be obtained
at www.ICGtesting.com
Printed in the USA
FFOW04n2029021017
40439FF

9 780692 608098